THE NEW ABBEY GIRLS

by

ELSIE J. OXENHAM

THE CHILDREN'S PRESS
LONDON AND GLASGOW

First printed in this edition 1966

PRINTED AND MADE IN GREAT BRITAIN

CONTENTS

CHAPTER I

MORNING IN THE ABBEY

"I WON'T! I won't go! And if you ask her to have me, I'll run away!" and scarlet with anger, her face working with distress, Maidlin rushed away into the abbey and hid herself in a corner.

Ann Watson, the caretaker, turned to her washing with pinched lips and worried face. It was only a week since this tempestuous niece had come to stay with her, but what a week it had been! Maidlin had been quiet enough and even reverent in her attitude to the beautiful old ruins, loving them and wondering at them, and wandering much among them, fascinated by her aunt's stories of the white-robed monks of long ago. But so much had happened in that week of Maidlin's visit! For Maidlin had suddenly become a person of consequence, and Ann hardly felt able to cope with the situation. And what was worse, the child had unexpectedly developed a temper, which had not shown at first, and Ann felt very decidedly that she did not know how to deal with her.

Maidlin had no mother, and her home had always been with her other aunt, who was married to a well-to-do farmer away in the north. This aunt's sudden illness had brought about the visit to Aunt Ann, who looked after Joan's Abbey of Grace-Dieu, and told visitors all about the Cistercians, and the destruction of the abbey, and its rescue by Sir Antony of the Hall.

As she washed, Ann's mind ran over the familiar story and she glanced through her lancet windows at the sunny garth, her troubled eyes seeing in memory what they might never, perhaps, see again in fact—two bronze-haired girls dancing minuets or morris jigs on the turf. "Princess

Royal," "Jockie," "Ladies' Pleasure"; Ann knew them all by name. But those days were over, she feared. For yesterday had been Joan's wedding-day, and the Hall had been astir with guests all afternoon. Now it was quiet again, the bride and bridegroom were far away, and every one was filled with sympathy for the lonely cousin left behind. What would Joy do without Joan? Even Ann wondered that. They had been together all their lives.

"She'll be lonely!" Ann said to herself. "Not at once, perhaps, because of Miss Jen. But when Miss Jen goes home"—and Ann shook her head doubtfully.

Ann knew Jen well, and had known her since Jen had begun her schooldays, five years ago, as a thirteen-year-old visitor to the Hall during its term as the headquarters of the school. She was glad Jen was to stay for a few days. Then her thoughts turned from weddings and the past to the problem of the moment, and she sighed and knit her brows again as she bent over her tub.

Three days ago the letter had come, from Maidlin's father in Italy. He was not in Italy just now, it appeared, but in China, and China seemed a very long way off, very much farther than Italy, which, to Ann, had always seemed far enough. And the letter, with its amazing news and its awkward suggestions, had disturbed Ann greatly. What to do about it, and how to start, she did not know. Only one solution had occurred to her, but she had thought it a very good one. But, as if the letter and its problems had not been enough, on top of it all Maidlin had most unexpectedly developed this "Italian" temper, unsuspected until now, and had flatly and very violently refused to consider Ann's solution of the difficulty for a single moment. Ann sighed again, and thought and thought, but could see no other way.

From somewhere in the abbey ruins came a high, clear voice, singing cheerfully an old jingle.

Ann smiled. "Miss Joy's keepin' up her spirits!" she said approvingly, and looked out to see the singer.

From the old doorway of the tresaunt, the passage leading to the abbots' garden and the gate into the grounds of the Hall, another verse peeled fourth.

Joy was talking cheerfully to herself. "This won't get my letters written! Bother weddings! Bother being an heiress and boss of an estate! It's more worry than it's worth!"

The broken arches of the cloisters had wide, low sills of grey stone. Joy spread papers, letters, envelopes and pad about, and laid a stone on each to keep them steady. From Joan's sanctum opening off the cloisters, she brought a cushion, and throwing it down on the stone sat upon it, her back against the wall, and set to work, humming all the time.

Ann, at her window a few yards away, smiled as she looked at her. "Miss Joy don't even begin to grow up! Now why that Maidlin should have such a spite at her is more than I can tell! A bit wild, Miss Joy used to be; but I'm sure these last few months she's been different somehow—kinder, and more gentle spoken like. But she don't look grown up this morning, and that's a fact!"

It was a fact. In spite of her twenty-one years, to which she only referred when she wanted an argument for getting her own way, she was wearing an old blue gym tunic, reaching to her knees.

So, writing-pad propped on the knees of her gym stockings, she leaned against the cloister wall and scribbled answers to the pile of letters, murmuring a comment now and then.

"Oh, what cheek! Begging letters are the limit! I will *not* give to everybody who asks, just because I've got the money! I'd have nothing left in three months! Oh, this this is from Miss Macey. I wonder what the old dear wants? Perhaps it's just more good wishes for Joan, come rather late. No, it's for me all right. Oh—help!"

She read the letter from her old schoolmistress, her merry face growing serious; then laid it down and sat staring across the garth at the high refectory windows.

"This needs some thinking about! *Dear* old Mackums! She's fearfully apologetic and all the rest of it, but she does know what she wants. Hi, Jenny-Wren! Come here and give me good advice! I know you're looking for me. Now don't begin cheering me up!" she threatened. "For I don't need it. I know you've all made up your minds to cheer me up, but you needn't bother, thank you! I can get along quite well without Joan!"

"I can't!" Jen came across the garth to join her. "I haven't come to cheer you up. I've come to be bucked up myself. I've no time to think about you! What do you suppose Joan's doing now? Where will they have got to?"

"They're doing the sights of Paris, my child, and have forgotten our existence. You needn't be sentimental over Joan; you know what she's like when Jack's round," Joy mocked. "There isn't anybody else, if she's got him!"

"He's worse. Nobody else exists, if Joan's there. Of course, it's awfully nice, and all that; and I'm glad they've got married. But I do feel left alone and lost. Isn't the morning after a wedding a horrible time?"

"Let's talk about the weather!" Joy suggested kindly. "Isn't it wonderfully mild for March? Feels like June, doesn't it? Awfully fortunate for the wedding! But, of course, the abbey's sheltered by the hills; it may be cold enough up on top! We shall soon have the blossom out, at this rate!"

"Joy, you're a pig! And you do look a sight! Do go and get dressed!"

"Soon. I want to consult you on a matter of serious importance first. Business must be attended to, Jenny-Wren. I've had a letter from Mackums."

"Oh! Does she want me to go over and see her? Why didn't she write to me?"

"It isn't about you at all. It's about quite another little girl, an infant of fifteen, called Rosamund Kane."

"Never heard of her. Who is she?"

"She's left on Mackums' tender hands as a boarder, while

her folks are abroad. Her relations live away up in the north, like yours, and aren't any use to this kid. And Wycombe doesn't suit her; she's lived in the north too, and she isn't well."

"Oh, but she'll get used to it! That's only for the first week," Jen said, from experience. "I always used to flop for a few days, and moon round with a headache, and say I'd never do any work. But it went off, and I was all right for the rest of the term."

"This kid has had two terms of it and it hasn't gone off, and Mackums is worried about her. Wycombe's so much among the hills."

"Yes, it's different out here. Better ask the kid—oh, is that what Miss Macey wants? Has she asked you to have the kid here?"

"That's exactly and precisely what she has done, Jenny-Wren. She's frightfully apologetic, and all that, but she knows we've heaps of room and everything, and she says, could we possibly have the kid here for a few months, so that she could live in country air and cycle to school every day? Mackums thinks it would be the making of her."

"It would be topping for the kid," Jen said slowly. "I haven't forgotten how you took me in, and were so awfully decent to me. What shall you do, Joy?"

"I don't know. I'm still thinking."

"You've been awfully good already, asking people here for holidays, because you thought they needed a rest in the country. Joan told me about it."

"I've had a queer feeling"—Joy began, and paused. "I'm going to tell you about it some time. But at this particular moment, what about Rosamund?"

"It does need thinking about," Jen acknowledged. "I wish we'd got Joan; she always knew!"

"I could write for advice to everybody," Joy mocked. "But I think it would be better to decide for myself. If I let the kid come here, it's I who will have to take the worry of her. But it does complicate matters."

"Not half!" Jen agreed, and sat on the grass, leaning against Joy's knee and frowning over the problem.

At eighteen, she was tall and slim and lithe. The yellow hair she had always worn in long plaits had been cut short after her accident the previous summer, and, discovering the comfort of a crown of bobbed curls, Jen had stoutly refused, for the present, to let it grow again. She wore it caught back from her face with a slide, and was happy in the freedom of the prevailing fashion. In her jumper and short skirt she still looked a schoolgirl, except for her height.

They sat thinking over their problem, Joy leaning back against the old grey stone of her cloister arch and nursing one knee, Jen propped against her sitting on the grass. Suddenly the clanging of the great abbey bell brought them both to their feet.

"It's only eleven o'clock," said Joy. "We aren't open till twelve. Ann won't let the idiots in. Go and tell her to send them for a walk in the woods for an hour, there's a good kid!"

"Here she comes! She wants to ask you something."

"Please, Miss Joy, it's a lady, and she says she's a friend of yours."

The girls looked at one another. "Who on earth——?"

"I'll go and see, shall I?" and Jen raced away across the garth.

Joy hastily began to gather up her scattered papers. "Whoever can it be? Is it anybody I'm prepared to receive in this—er—costume? There aren't very many! But Jen will know," and she withdrew towards the door of the private room in the cloister wall, ready to take cover, if necessary.

"Jen's excited about it, whoever it is. I can hear her shrieks from here. She always did give a yell and hurl herself on people," and Joy chuckled.

Jen came flying back. "Joy! Oh, you needn't hide! You really needn't! It's Madam!" and Jen collapsed in laughter on the grass. "Fancy hiding from *her*, because you're in your tunic! "

"Idiot!" Joy hurled at her, and went leaping across the garth, all long, flying legs, to the tunnel passage and the old front gate.

CHAPTER II

ENTER MADAM

"BUT we thought you were teaching in Oxford last night! You said so at the wedding yesterday!" Joy was remonstrating, as she gave joyful welcome to this, their first teacher at the Cheltenham folk-dancing school, and a friend now of many months.

"So I was," Madam said imperturbably. "I had classes all evening. But I thought I'd give you a surprise, and I wanted to see the abbey again."

"But we asked you to come, and you said you had to get back to town for classes this morning? "

"They've got measles in the school. So they wired me, and I've got the morning off. I can't go back till they're out of quarantine, of course."

"Oh, that's wonderful! Can you stop a few days?"

"Oh, I've a town class to-night; three, in fact; and a lecture by the Director afterwards, and I've got to sing. But I've the morning off, so I came back to give you a shock."

"You did it! Several shocks. But it's lovely to have you here."

"Busy person!" said Jen. "She shall sing to us, to your piano, Joy. She can practise for to-night."

Madam laughed. "Are you trying to pretend it's last Vacation School, or preparing for next?" she asked of Joy.

"Oh, I often fly round like this in mornings. I'll run you down to Wycombe in Belinda after lunch."

"Will you? I'd love it! But my bag's down at the station. I walked up through the woods, by the beech path."

"We'll pick it up as we go."

"I'd love to be whirled down to Wycombe, instead of going all the way round by train," Madam said warmly.

"You're a sport! I won't smash you up, honestly. I know I'd have to reckon with somebody if I did!"

"Where is your husband, by the way?" Jen said reproachfully.

"Oh, he went back to town last night. We didn't know to-day was to be a holiday, or I might have let him stay. When are you coming to town to see his book? He's doing one, just like yours, you know."

"What do you mean? Nobody could make a book like these now," Joy argued, as they stood in the refectory by the big cases which held the manuscripts discovered in the secret chamber under the abbey.

"He could. He's doing one. You must come and see it. Of course, it will take years to finish it. I'd like you to see it. It's really rather good." Madam was turning over the leaves of a missal with careful fingers but critical eyes, her studiously-off-hand tone holding only the faintest suggestion of pride in her husband's beautiful work. "He's been at it for years already. It's going to be shown at an exhibition soon, but if you come in time you shall have a private view."

"Oh, we'll come!" Joy said warmly. "I'm going up to town one day soon!"

"Just let me know when you're coming. I'm out a great deal, you know," said Madam.

"Would you consider me a fit and proper guardian for an infant of fourteen, to set it a good example and bring it up in the way it should go?" Joy asked suddenly, while they were still poring over the beautiful old illuminated sheets.

"The very last person in the world I should choose. Why?" Madam asked absently, intent on a fourteenth-century book of prayers. "Who is the infant you want to be guardian to? I'm not so sure; perhaps I'm wrong. I haven't seen very much of you lately," and she gave her a keen, thoughtful look."

"Oh, I quite agree with you! It's just how I feel myself. And I don't want to do it a scrap."

"It would be a great chance for the child, of course. But it would mean some responsibility for you," Madam said thoughtfully, when she understood the position.

"It all needs some thinking about—Help! What on earth is it?"

"Oh, you little wretch! How you made us jump!" Jen cried wrathfully, as a small figure fell rather than climbed down from the high niche which had once been the pulpit, or seat of the lay brother who read aloud during meal-times to the assembled monks.

"Is this your new ward?" and Madam, having recovered from the shock, turned to look curiously at the dishevelled little figure, dusty and untidy, with big black eyes and a cloud of wild black hair.

"The bell's gone! You didn't hear, you were talking so hard! Visitor-people, to see the abbey. Aren't you going to hide?"—to Joy. "But I don't believe you've time, unless aunty keeps them at the gate. I'll go"—and she whirled past them and down the winding stair in the wall.

"Gracious! It *is* after twelve! Then we can't say anything! We shall jolly well be caught this time!" Joy groaned, glancing hurriedly at her wrist-watch.

"Oh, couldn't we hide, as the child suggested?" Madam laughed. "Where do you generally go?"

"Through the chapter-house!" Jen laughed. "We'll go home by Underground, Joy!"

"Come on!" said Madam, eager as a schoolgirl for a joke or a new experience.

"Don't fall and twist your ankle!" Jen warned Madam. "The steps are frightfully uneven. There! That's safe!"

They could not have crossed the garth unseen. Already Ann's voice could be heard, "reciting dates, "as Jen murmured, to the tourists. But it only took a second for them all to slip into the chapter-house, which stood at right angles to the refectory. Joy, delighting in the freedom of her costume, took a flying vault through the low window at the inner end, and Jen followed as swiftly and easily. They both turned to give their hands to their guest, but found her already on the sill; she took Jen's hand and sprang lightly down, and they all vanished into the tunnel of the secret passage, through the old carved door.

"I'd forgotten your flying leaps on to forms and chairs!" Joy laughed. "I was going to apologise for asking you to climb through windows, but perhaps I needn't."

"Oh, don't trouble! But you abbey people are so unexpected!" and Madam paused on the steps to laugh. "Have we a light? Or do we sit in the dark?"

"I keep a torch in a hidie-hole, for fear of accidents," and Joy burrowed in the dark, and flashed on an electric torch, while Jen closed the outer door. "It's not the first time I've taken cover here! Do you want to see the crypt and the well again? Or shall we go straight home to lunch?"

"Oh, I think we might just have a minute down there. I'd like to see the abbot's tomb again."

"Right-o! I do know a little about this, if Joan left anything out when you came before," and Joy led the way down the steps.

CHAPTER III

BURIED ALIVE

"Be careful here!" and Joy paused in the passage behind the stairs. "Do you draw the line at planks over bottomless pits?"

"*What?*" Madam peered over her shoulder. "What has happened down here? There were no bottomless pits when I came in January."

"It went all boggy and squishy in that heavy rain just after the President's wedding, and we decided there must be an underground spring, like the one you fall into on the upper path. So Joan said it had better be drained, and it was a bigger job than they expected. It isn't finished yet. I don't say the hole's bottomless, but it's rather deep, so don't fall off the plank. Do you mind?"

"Not so long as there's a light," Madam laughed, and followed her across a couple of uneven boards bridging a deep chasm.

Then Jen gave a shriek of dismay. "Joy. The torch is going out!"

"Help! What on earth shall we do?" gasped Joy, and stared helplessly at the light, which gave a last feeble flicker and went out.

For a moment there was silence in the old church, the blank silence of underground—"Of a tomb." as Jen said later. Then Madam's laugh rang out. "*Well*, Joy Shirley! Of all the ways to treat your visitors! Didn't I say you abbey people were unexpected? I suppose you know your way out by this time?"

"Oh, I know my way!" Joy said gloomily. "And I'll get you out, if I have to go on my hands and knees all the way. But it won't be easy; *you* can't crawl across planks!"

"I'd forgotten the bottomless pit!" Madam sobered hastily. "That's another story. You can't cross those planks without a light, Joy. I won't allow it. We'll wait——"

"You and Jen must wait, of course. We're not all three going to crawl! But I'm going to get out somehow and bring back a light for you."

"Joy, don't be silly!" Madam's voice had its old note of authority. "There are visitors in the abbey. Won't the woman bring them here? Surely she'll have a light?"

"Saved!" Jen cried dramatically. "Of course she will! We've only got to wait!"

"They're sure to come here, aren't they?" Madam insisted, as Joy still hesitated. "Very well, then. We'll wait. It would be awfully risky to try to cross that plank without a light. I never felt anything so solid as this blackness!"

"You always say you can see in the dark, Wild Cat!" Jen mocked to Joy. "Lead us to the tomb! I say! Doesn't it sound awful?"

"I'm frightfully sorry!" Joy apologised abjectly, as she guided them carefully through the blackness of the crypt. "Here you are! I say! " to Madam. "We don't often do this with our visitors!"

Madam felt her way carefully to a broad step, and with equal care sat down upon it. Then she leant back against the big square table-tomb and began to laugh, and laughed till she nearly cried. "I'll *never* forget it! I *never* expected to be buried alive! Joy Shirley, you'll never hear the end of this!"

"I know," Joy agreed ruefully. "I never shall."

"I nearly *died* when the light went out!" and Madam went off into another peal of laughter. "Jen's shriek—and the last glimpse of your horror-stricken face—and the picture of you crawling along those planks—and the silence and darkness you can *feel*!"

"They may not come," Joy said gloomily. "Perhaps it's only some old ladies. If Ann tells them about the pit and the planks, they won't trouble to come down."

"Oh, I think they'll look down, whoever they are, and

we'll all yell together at the slightest sound!" Jen argued. "Besides, there's a man. I saw him as I scooted into the chapter-house. He won't mind planks! He'll want to see where the jewels were found!"

"It's frightfully ignominious to sit waiting to be rescued by a strange man!" and Madam's voice shook.

"Now don't you go off again!" Jen pleaded. "Do you ever have hysterics?"

"No, *never*! But I've never been buried alive before. Anything may happen! Joy, don't you really think it's funny?"

Joy surrendered, and began to laugh. "Oh, if you don't mind! But I am awfully sorry——"

"You've got to amuse me!" Madam said peremptorily. "I'm not going to sit here in the depths doing nothing! Tell me something interesting! What did you mean by what you said in the refectory, Jenny-Wren, when that child fell out of the pulpit on to us like a bomb? You called her 'the novelette girl'?"

"That's what Joy calls her. Her name's Madalena di Ravarati."

"But who or what is she?"

"Our good caretaker is her aunt," Joy explained. "Ann calls her Maidlin, and so does everybody else; I believe it's old English for Magdalene. She's lived with another aunt in the north, who always called her Maidlin."

"Maidlin! It's pretty. So is she, I should think, when you see her properly. She had beautiful dark eyes, and a lovely clear skin. Surely she's partly Italian?"

"That's the novelette bit, of course. About twenty years ago Ann was nurse in a family in London; and she had a little sister, heaps younger, who came up from the country to be a housemaid in the same place. And this sister, Mary, was very pretty. A visitor at the house, apparently an Italian, fell in love with the pretty housemaid. Finally he and Mary went out one day and were married. He took Mary away to the other sister, the one who has brought Maidlin up, and wrote to his people to break the news. They were furious, and told him to come home at once, but not to dare to bring his wife. He wouldn't go without her; but it got on her mind, and at last, she begged him to go and try to get things settled up more happily. He gave in and went, meaning to be back before the baby was born. But Mary was taken ill suddenly, and she died, and he never saw her again. Maidlin was a tiny scrap of a thing, and her aunt had hard work to save her life. Her father came to see her, but he couldn't forgive himself for having gone away at all. He didn't know what to do with the kid, so he left her with the aunt, and sent money quite regularly for her to be properly brought up."

"And is he still alive?" asked Madam. "Does he ever come to see the child?"

"Ann says he's got some kind of post abroad. He does come, but he hasn't been for some years now. Just at present the Cumberland aunt is ill, so Maidlin is stopping with Ann. And we call her the novelette girl. Do you wonder?"

"I don't blame you! And she'll go back to Cumberland when the aunt is better?"

"Oh, yes, I guess so! I say, aren't you getting chilly?"

"A bit," Madam assented: "Sit up close, both of you. We'll huddle together to keep warm. Hasn't anybody any chocolate? I've a whole packet in my bag at the station; and a pound of apples!"

"A lot of use that is!" Jen jeered.

"Joy ought to keep a secret store down here, if she means to bury her visitors often. You should have laid in provisions before you cut off our retreat, Joy."

"I shall never hear the end of it!" Joy groaned.

"No, you never will. I shall tell everybody; every single person I meet! Get up, Joy!" Madam said peremptorily. "You've sat there long enough. Tunics aren't made for sitting on damp stones in."

"No, it's coming through," and Joy stood up and shook herself. "But what can I do? Jump?"

"You might do capers," Jen began to laugh. "Try uprights, Joy. Your kick-jumps are still awful. Don't kick us, though! Pity Madam can't criticise!"

"Do 'Princess Royal' in the dark!" Madam suggested, laughter in her voice again.

"It serves you right, Joy!" Jen teased.

"I'll do 'Princess Royal' on the spot. Sing the tune for me!" Joy demanded.

Madam, really anxious lest she should have taken a chill, complied, and criticised the sound of the feet at the end. "You lost your rhythm once or twice. Are you warmer now?"

"You bet! Trust a morris jig for that. I've done 'Princess Royal' a good many times, but never in quite such a queer place before!"

"Now 'Molly Oxford,' Joy!" said Madam. "That's almost all on one spot."

Joy defiantly began to dance again. "I wish you could see! I'm really doing a very beautiful jig! You'd better have a go too. It's awfully warming!" she suggested.

"What a picture for our rescuers!" Madam began to laugh. "No, we'll be the orchestra. What would you like now?"

"Sing me 'Trunkles.' I want to practise my galleys," Joy demanded.

Madam, with a suppressed chuckle, was complying, when Jen gave a wild yell. "Help! Help! Come to the rescue! Come and save us, *please*!"

"At last! And I was just doing such a *beautiful* galley!" Joy said resentfully. "Coo-ee!" and she shouted through her hands. "Shall we go to meet them?"

Ann, bewildered by the shouts and not recognising the voices in the enclosed space, came first across the planks, looking distinctly frightened. Joy and Jen were upon her in a moment, explaining at express speed what had happened, both talking at once, forgetful of everything else.

Madam's amused eyes found the astonished visitor in the background. He was tall and grave, and his questioning gaze went from one to the other of the excited girls, and rested longest on Joy, in her very short tunic and the rolled-up hair. The bright bronze hair betrayed her as plainly as a label, for everyone had heard of the red-haired girls who owned the abbey and the Hall, and he had just heard the whole story from Ann.

His look was so incredulous that Madam chuckled again. Then she rose and went forward with the dignity she knew so well how to assume. "Thank you! We were without a light, so had to wait till you came."

"Oh!" Jen's eyes had just fallen on the stranger.

Joy became conscious of his presence at the same moment. "We'll go home to lunch. Perhaps you will hold the light while we cross the planks," she said haughtily.

"Allow me!" and the stranger took the light from Ann, and, crossing the plank, turned to give his hand to each as she followed.

Madam accepted his help graciously, with calm dignity and no sign of inward amusement. Joy stalked across haughtily, not seeming to see the offered hand. Jen, with an admiring eye on Madam, tried to imitate her gracious manner, clutched his hand, and nearly fell into the hole.

"Gracious, Jenny-Wren! You might as well have crossed in the dark!" Madam mocked. "Don't go and fall in now, after waiting nearly an hour to be rescued!"

"Had you been imprisoned there so long?" the tourist turned to Joy in dismay.

"We'd been there about a week," Jen informed him. "We were dancing about to keep warm; Joy was, at least."

Madam's hand on her arm restrained her from more indiscretions. "Thank you! We can have no difficulty now. Here are the steps. I'm hungry! I shall eat grass in a moment! Aren't you going to feed me, Joy? You said something about a very big lunch. Couldn't we run?" and Madam cast dignity to the winds, and raced, with Jen leading the way, across the garth to the tresaunt entrance and so to the old gate into the gardens of the Hall.

Joy gave a despairing look round, then followed, all long legs and flying girdle. "I don't suppose you two lunatics saw that severe old lady sitting waiting in the cloisters? No, I thought you hadn't! She'll spread the most awful stories of lunatics at large in the abbey. Why couldn't you be dignified for two minutes longer?" indignantly to Madam. "You can put it on so jolly well when you like!"

"No, really? An old lady? I never saw her. Shall I go back and apologise, on your behalf?" Madam teased.

"It would only be you she disapproved of, Joy. Oh, don't let's go back! I'm simply dying of hunger," Jen wailed.

"I suppose you know the President has given you a new name since you got married?" Joy queried, as she locked the garden gate behind them.

"Me? No, what?" Madam demanded.

"She calls you The Duchess," Joy said grimly. "Because of the grand manner you put on now and then."

"It's the way she walks, somehow! I can't think how she does it!" Jen sighed.

"Not when she's tearing madly across cloister garths, I suppose!" Madam teased. "I'll tell the President what I think of her next time she comes to see me. And when you come," to Joy, "I shall be very forgiving and do my best not to lose you underground!"

"I shall never hear the end of it!" Joy sighed, as they reached the house. "Aunty, dear! We've brought The Duchess home to lunch!"

CHAPTER IV

THE NOVELETTE GIRL

WHEN Madam, laden with almond-blossom and daffodils for her London flat, had been tucked into Belinda's sidecar and whirled away down to Wycombe to catch the afternoon train, Jen returned to the abbey for the letters and papers left there in the morning.

Ann had them in safe keeping; as she handed them over; she asked anxious questions about the morning's adventure, and Jen explained just what had happened.

As she talked, Ann listened in dismay and tried to express her regret that they had had to wait so long. The gentleman and the old lady had been greatly interested in the ruins, it appeared, and had asked questions which had seemed endless. They had left a card, with a request that it be given to Miss Shirley, so Ann handed it to Jen, whose lips pursed in a whistle of dismay as she read the names.

"Help! Those people! Joy won't like that!" she said softly, under her breath.

"I was wanting a word with Miss Joy," Ann's voice was nervous and hesitating as she broke in on Jen's worried thinking. "Would it do if I came up to the Hall to-night, Miss Jen?"

"Help! Is Ann going to give notice? What next? Poor old Joy! Everything's going wrong at once!" Jen's lips tightened again. "That will be all right, Ann. She's only gone for a run on her bike. She'll be home to tea," and she turned to cross the garth soberly. "Between Miss Macey's school kid, and these new people turning up at such an awkward time, and Ann giving notice—if that's what she wants with Joy!—things don't look like being so awfully flat, after all. Oh, there's the novelette girl!"

She paused beside a little figure curled up in a corner, in an angle between two grey walls. She stood over the child and said warmly, "Thank you for giving us warning this morning! It was jolly decent of you to think of it."

"What's she been saying to you?" said Maidlin suspiciously.

"Who? Your aunt? Nothing. We spoke about this morning, and she said she wanted to talk business with Joy and she'd come to the Hall this evening."

"I knew she would!" and Maidlin was on her feet with a bound. "I told her!"—and she sped across the garth and hurled herself into Ann's little kitchen.

"Well!" Jen murmured, and stood staring after her. "What on earth's the matter with the kid? She is like a novelette, more and more!" and she went home by way of the tresaunt and garden, pondering this strange development in their guest.

"I say 'Traveller's Joy!'" and at the first sound of Belinda's horn, Jen went flying to the door. "Come in here at once! What umpteen years you've been! I've three thrilling things to tell you!"

Joy came stalking in in her leather coat and breeches. "Three thrilling things! I've had adventures by the way, too. Coming home, just outside the abbey gates, I almost committed murder; no, on second thoughts, I think any jury would have acquitted me *this* time, anyway. They'd have brought in a verdict of suicide, probably whilst of unsound mind."

"What are you talking about, silly?" Jen laughed. "Did you run over a hen?"

Joy, sitting on the big oak settle, said scornfully, "Hen? No, my child. I nearly killed Madalena di Ravarati."

"Oh!" Jen sat back on her heels and stared up at her. "Oh, was she flying out of the house in a rage?"

"In a towering temper—a real Italian passion, I should say. Never saw me coming, of course, but dashed headlong into the road. I just managed to avoid running her down;

then, when I turned to swear at her, I saw she was galloping down the road at about a thousand miles an hour; no hat —slippers—overall on—hair all flying; looked a perfect lunatic!"

Jen chuckled. "I suppose you went after Maidlin?"

"Rather! She tried to dodge, but of course I got her, and dumped her in the car and brought her back, and tried to find out what it was all about. But by that time she'd collapsed, and was crying herself sick; I really thought she'd be ill on my hands. So I raced her home and handed her over to Ann, and said I'd hear all about the row later on."

"I saw the beginning of it," said Jen. "I don't know yet what the row's all about, but that's one of my three thrilling things—Madalena's Italian temper. I spoke to her on the garth, and she flared up, just like gunpowder! But you'll know all about it soon, Joy, for Ann's coming along to talk business with you after closing time; that's the second thing. I thought at first she was going to give notice, but by the way Maidlin went off with a whizz-bang when I happened to mention it, I think now perhaps it had something to do with her. She said—'I knew she would! I told her!' and went flying off to have a scene with Ann. I suppose Maidlin got the worst of it, and went tearing off down the road in a rage."

"And barged into me and Belinda! What a queer business!" and Joy sat looking worried.

"It isn't quite the last straw, though," Jen said ruthlessly. "I hope you can stand one more shock. Who do you suppose those people were this morning?"

Joy stared at her amazedly. "Who? Oh, the tourists in the crypt?"

"Yes, but they weren't tourists, unfortunately. That's the point." Jen handed her the card. "The new people from the Manor! Such a way to get introduced to your new next-door neighbours!"

"What?" Joy stared at the card, then hurled it from her across the hall. "Oh, I say! That is rotten luck! What will they think of us? I don't care for myself, but I know Joan and aunty wanted to be friends."

"It is annoying!" Jen said soothingly. "But we can't alter it now. Come and have some more tea, Joy. And after that you've got to write your letters, and I must finish mine to Cicely. What shall you say to Miss Macey about her kid—Rosamund, isn't it?"

Joy frowned. "I'll wait till I've seen Ann before I decide. If she should give notice and leave the abbey on my hands, I don't see that I can take on anything more till I've fixed up with someone else. But if it isn't that, or if Ann's got any more worries for me, about Madalena or any one else—well—I shall burst into tears! There'll be nothing else to do. And after that I shall be driven to take a very drastic step!" Joy said dramatically. "I was thinking about it when I nearly ran over Maidlin. I won't tell you what it's going to be yet, but I'm coming to see it's the only thing to do. If things get any worse, you'll see!"

CHAPTER V

ANN'S REQUEST

THE big lounge hall of Joy's house was a very attractive place, with its oak-panelled walls and family portraits, big stained-glass windows, polished floor, big rugs, Joy's beautiful piano, and daffodils on each of the old tables in big blue bowls and vases. Mrs. Shirley was resting after the excitements of the last few days, and preferred to stay in her own little sitting-room upstairs, but the girls loved the hall and used it whenever they were indoors.

Each annexing a wide window-seat, they spread their letters in earnest.

"Yes, Ann? What is it?" Joy's voice roused Jen to sudden interest.

She laid down her pad. "Is it business, Ann? Shall I go away?"

"Sit down, Ann." Joy had laid aside her writing with relief. "No, don't budge, Jenny-Wren. I may want your support, if the worst comes to the worst."

"It's about Maidlin, Miss Joy," Ann began nervously.

"Oh! How can I help?"

"There's a letter from her father, miss, and—and I don't right know what to do." Ann's nervousness increased as she went on.

"He do say, Miss Joy," and Ann's correct English forsook her in her excitement, "he do say as how his old father and mother be both dead of the 'flu and all the money, what they wouldn't let him have any of, because of him getting married to our Mary, it's all to belong to our Maidlin, the money, and the houses, and the horses and carriages and the motors, and the pictures, and all," and Ann gazed at Joy with incredulous, half-frightened eyes.

" 'Tis some old will," Ann was fumbling in her pocket for the letter. "I'll show you what he says, Miss Joy. I thought you'd tell me what to do. His father said he'd leave him out of the money altogether, so he made it that every mortal thing must go to his grandchildren, for he'd got two, a boy and a girl, and our Maidlin not being born then, nor thought of, you understand. But the girl, she died at school; and the boy were killed in the war; and there aren't any more, nor any one left to say it isn't fair."

"And the will was never changed! They'd never seen Maidlin, of couse, and they were getting very old, and they forgot her existence," Joy said excitedly. "Well, Ann, what are you going to do now? Is he coming to fetch Madalena? For if she's a great heiress, she'll want educating, and all kinds of things."

Ann's strange nervousness returned, and she stammered and hesitated. "Her father, he writes as he can't come home all at once, for he's away in Chiny, and the folks there, what give him a job when he needed it bad, they be in the middle o' some work o' some kind, and sort of depending on him, and he says 'twould ruin it if he come away just now, and he can't chuck things up all at once. He'll come just as soon as he can get away, he says, but things is difficult and unsettled in that part o' Chiny, and he don't know quite when 'twill be."

"I see. It is awkward for him," Joy agreed. "Well? What does he want done with Maidlin in the meantime? Are you to send her to Italy?"

"That would be awfully hard on the kiddy!" Jen urged. "She can't speak a word of French, let alone Italian, for I asked her."

"That's what he says, Miss Jen," Ann spoke eagerly. "No, he says, will we keep her till he can come and take her home himself. And he says, could we send her to a good school for a little while, or—or get her a place to live with—with nice people, who'd know what she ought to learn, and teach her, so's she'd be ready when he comes."

"That's a very good idea," Joy said warmly. "Not a school, though, I think. In a school she'd only be one of a crowd of girls. But a nice family, where they knew the story and understood just what she needed;—yes, that's what you want. How will you find the right place, Ann? You must be very particular where you send her. Could I make any inquiries for you? Miss Macey might——"

"Joy, don't you see?" Jen spoke softly. To her eyes, gifted with insight which Joy had never learned, it was plain enough. The pathetic pleading in Ann's eyes spoke for itself. Jen saw plainly what was in her mind, but how Joy would take it she was not sure. "Joy, she wants you to have Maidlin here."

"My hat!" gasped Joy. "I hadn't thought of that!" and she stared aghast at the caretaker.

"I—I know I hadn't ought to think of it, Miss Joy," Ann faltered. "But 'twould be the making of the child, and—and I don't know what to do. *I* ain't fit to look after her now!"

Joy sat biting her lips and staring out at the lawn. Jen watched her anxiously.

"Well, neither am I!" Joy burst out at last. "Fit to look after her, I mean. You want me to take your kid, who knows absolutely nothing, and train her for you till she's fit to take her proper place——"

"No, only till her father comes home!" Jen put in quickly. "It's only to start Maidlin properly. But I'm not saying you ought to do it. Of course, it would be a gorgeous thing for her, and all that, but there's no reason why you should do it, if you don't want to. If you could help Ann to find some other place, wouldn't that do just as well?"

"I could do that, of course. But I really don't feel I'm the proper person to bring Maidlin up for you!" Joy spoke eagerly and hopefully.

"I do ask your pardon for thinking of it, Miss Joy. I hadn't any right to say it. 'Twould be a trouble to you, I can see," Ann faltered apologetically.

Joy cut her short. "I'll think over all the likely people, and see if any of them could help, Ann. I'll come down and see you about it all in a day or two, when I've had time to think. In the meanwhile you'd better keep an eye on your heiress. I suppose you know I nearly killed her this afternoon? What was the matter with her?"

Ann, very red, would or could give no explanation.

As the door closed behind her, Jen burst out again, "Joy, don't you see? Maidlin doesn't want to be sent here. That's what she was so mad about this afternoon. She knew Ann was going to ask you to have her."

"Oh!" Joy said slowly. "Well, that settles it, of course. I wouldn't dream of having her if the very thought of coming here could put her in such a rage. But why, Jenny-Wren? What's the matter with her? Why won't she come here?" with a touch of indignation, as she in her turn looked round the hall.

Jen sat staring at her, her eyes very thoughtful. "I don't know. I don't know her well enough to say. But I know how I should feel in Maidlin's place. If I thought someone was going to be asked to have me; if I were Maidlin, and knew my aunt was coming up here to ask you to take me in; well I should simply hate it, that's all."

"Oh, I see!" Joy said slowly, and stared back at her with knitted brows. "Well, if I say I won't have her, she'll be quite pleased, and it will be all right."

"I suppose so," Jen spoke doubtfully. "That depends on whether she really wanted to come or not."

"I thought you just said she'd hate it!"

"I never did! I said she'd hate knowing her aunt had *asked* you to have her. She might be dying to come all the time. That would make it all the worse."

Joy pursed her lips, and stared out into the garden. "It's awfully hard on the kid! You can't wonder if she's all worked up. And she has nobody who can really help her. She jolly well needs somebody," and she sat staring out at the lawn, and the almond-blossom over the old orchard wall, the glimpse of the abbey ruins behind.

"Of course, I could do it. . . . Joan would have done it," she said at last.

"Yes, I think she would," Jen agreed. "But she wouldn't have taken on the job unless she'd meant to do it properly, Joy. I mean, if she'd agreed to have the kid here, she'd have done an awful lot for her. It's a very big thing to ask."

Joy lapsed into worried silence again. At last she spoke, and very definitely. "We'll tell aunty, of course; but she'll say I must do what I think right. There's nothing else for it! I've made up my mind! I'm going up to town to-morrow to have a heart-to-heart talk with the Pixie!"

"Oh!" Jen gave a subdued shriek of delight. "What a gorgeous idea! She'll talk some sense to us!"

CHAPTER VI

A DUMPING-GROUND FOR GIRLS

"YOU'D better ring up the Pixie and make sure she's in town," Jen suggested. "Half the time she isn't."

"She was getting back to-day. That's why she couldn't come to the wedding." Joy was absent and preoccupied.

"Ring up Jacky-boy, too, Joy, and say we'll stay the night with her. Then"—Jen's eyes kindled—"we could go to classes with her at night; she goes every Friday. Madam will have a fit if we turn up without any warning, especially after yesterday!"

"That's all right," Joy said presently. "Jacky-boy says our room is always ready for us, any old time we like to come, and there are classes. And the Pixie says, 'Good! Come to tea at my flat! *Won't* we talk!' So to-morrow's all planned out."

That night she drifted into Jen's bedroom, in her dressing-gown.

"May I sit on you? I want to talk."

"You may even brush your hair over me," Jen laughed.

"It's all your fault, Jenny-Wren!" Joy shook the shining veil over her face, and spoke vehemently.

"What's my fault? I'm sorry! What's the worry, Joy?"

"That I can't just say no to all these bothering people, and be done with it. I'd have done it a year ago, without thinking twice."

"Oh? But I don't see it! My fault? Why?"

"For nearly getting killed by me, and making me think about things seriously for the first time."

"Oh!" Jen said slowly. She sat up and clasped her knees, shaking back her yellow curls. "Tell me some more! I'm afraid I don't *quite* see it yet, Joy."

"I nearly killed you when I flung you out of Belinda, and at first we didn't know if you'd live or die," Joy said vehemently. "I suppose you know I nearly *died*?"

"It wasn't as bad as that, Joy! I'm so sorry you had such a rotten time. And I came quite all right again, after all."

"I was just a spoiled baby, up till that hideous time. And when you began to get better," Joy said swiftly, "I said to myself such a time should never come again. I'd been given another chance, and I'd use it properly. I'd do something worth-while, and make people feel it was worth having me around, instead of being no use to any one and just pleasing myself and having a good time. And because I was so awfully grateful that you were alive, I meant to be different and do decent things all the rest of my life. I'll never forget, and I'll never stop being thankful. Jenny-Wren, ever since that time at Cheltenham last August, I've been wondering what I could do that would be worth-while, because of my gladness at your coming back. I've heaps of money, and of course I want to use it well. And I've this gorgeous house, and it all feels too good for me. I'd never done anything to deserve it; it just came. I'm ashamed to be a worthless, useless, good-for-nothing, just pleasing myself."

"Joy, you aren't that! You've done heaps of good things for people."

"I've tried," Joy said swiftly. "I can't see anything else to do but to use the money and the house and everything for people who need help, to give them a good time. Seems to me the first thing is to use them properly. And I suppose 'properly' would be for other people. I may be all wrong, but that's how it looks to me."

"No, I think you're all right. But you have thought a lot about it, Joy!"

"I've been thinking all winter. I've talked a little to Joan and aunty, but not very much. I felt I ought to see it through for myself."

"Those people you've had here and given country holidays to," Jen said tentatively. "You were trying to use your house properly then, Joy? Joan told me how awfully grateful they'd all been."

"That was one little way I thought of. I saw girls at Cheltenham who were working too hard; dancing all through their holidays because they could get a better position if they had their certificates. I got their addresses from headquarters, and if they were anywhere near, I asked them out here for long week-ends. And how they loved it! It's an awfully silly little thing to do, but it does mean a lot to some of them."

"Then it isn't a silly little thing!" Jen retorted. "And thinking of it wasn't a silly little thing, either. I think it's just a wonderful thing to be able to do, Joy."

"I felt I could do it, and I'd be utterly mean, and a downright rotter, if I didn't. And really and truly, that's how I feel about Maidlin, and Miss Macey's girl, too," and Joy tossed back her hair and faced Jen defiantly. "I'll feel I'm a slacker if I refuse, and since last August I've tried not to be a slacker. But I may be all wrong. I don't feel sure of myself. So I'm going to town to have a heart-to-heart talk with the Pixie, for she's got the biggest share of matter-of-fact business-like common sense, mixed with the biggest supply of plain ordinary goodness and kindness, that I've ever met in anybody. She'll tell me what's what, and just what I ought to do. Now go to sleep, Jenny-Wren, and forget all my silly talking. But I wanted to unload it on to somebody; and I wanted you to know it was all your fault. Thank you for listening! I feel better!"

She was up early next morning, to make preparations for the trip to town. But Jen was even earlier, and met her in the entrance-hall, in her fur cap and coat, her arms full of willow-twigs covered with silvery balls. "I've been robbing your woods! If the Pixie lives at the top of a London house, as I've been told, don't you think she'd like some pussy-palm to remind her of the country?"

"The Duchess loved it yesterday. Yes, let's take all we

can carry. And daffodils from the orchard, and some almond in bud."

"My Jacky-boy will want some, too. Harley Street isn't exactly full of daffodils. We'd better take a good lot," and Jen went to examine the letters on the round table.

"One for you from home. The usual stacks for me," and Joy dropped on a window-seat in the early sunshine with her budget.

A cry from Jen made her look up quickly. "What's the matter? Anything wrong?"

"Father isn't well again, and—it's awfully hard on you, Joy! I know you won't mind, but it does seem as if everybody were making you a dumping-ground for girls all at once! Mother wonders if you could put up with me here for two or three weeks, because he may have to come up to London for treatment, and it's a pity for me to go home and have to come back again. Can you put up with me?" and Jen stood looking down at her with a comical expression of dismay and apology.

"Cheers! Oh, cheers! You know I'm glad to have you, Jenny-Wren! Will you stay with me all the time?"

"Oh, no! Only till they get settled somewhere in town. Mother will come with him, and there won't be anybody left at home. I couldn't live there all alone, and mother and father will want me to be with them. But till they get settled, Joy——!"

"Keep them unsettled as long as ever you can, Jenny-Wren! I shan't consider them settled till they've bought and furnished a house in town."

"And I'll see how you get on with the novelette girl, and Miss Macey's kid! They'll be able to amuse one another, anyway, Joy. Mother's going to tell me definitely in a few days if they are coming, but she wanted me to consult you."

"Tell her I'm delighted, and overjoyed, and honoured; and the longer you can stop with me the more delighted and overjoyed and honoured I shall be. But if you chuck me and go and stop with Jacqueline in town, I won't forgive you in a hurry!"

"I know Jacky-boy would have me," Jen laughed. "If you and I quarrel, I can always run away to her. But I do love the abbey and the Hall."

"I'm just frightfully glad to think you'll be here a little longer!" Joy said warmly.

CHAPTER VII

CONSULTING THE PIXIE

"WE'LL go in Eirene," said Joy, at lunch-time. "It seems rude to dear Belinda not to let her have a run to town, but considering the amount of pussy-willow and daffodils Jen's taking along with her, Eirene seems necessary."

And when the girls set out, in the little car which for longer journeys had taken the motor-cycle's place in Joy's affections, the back seat was heaped with flowers and catkins and blossom.

"Where are we going first, Wild Cat?" Jen asked.

Joy glanced at her watch. "The Little One's expecting us early. She said 'three o'clockish,' and it's three now. We're not to be late, for she has to go out. So we're all out for the Pixie's flat. Now, don't chatter, my infant! I've got to keep an eye on the traffic. I don't want to kill you a second time."

Jen subsided, and watched in admiring silence as the strong hands gripped the wheel, the keen eyes watched carefully.

"You're an awfully good driver, Joy," she said seriously, when they were held up for a moment by a policeman at Oxford Circus.

"I've had the fright of my life," Joy said grimly. "I don't want another. Now we're off! We're almost there."

"Oh, does the Pixie live here?" said Jen as Eirene pulled up before a block of high, straight-fronted houses in a wide, quiet street just off a busy thoroughfare, filled with vans and buses, motors, and wagons.

"Shares a flat with two more, but she said they'd be out. Come and disentangle your pussy-palm! Its fingers are all tied up in knots."

"It looks awfully dull and—and grey, and uninteresting!" Jen said doubtfully. "And she loves pretty things."

"You wouldn't ask her to have her house green and blue and yellow outside, would you?" Joy mocked. "Perhaps inside it's more like her. Let's go up! I'll tootle to give her warning," and she woke the echoes with Eirene's horn.

The bare stone staircase, of wide, shallow steps, up which they climbed flight after flight to the top, depressed Jen still more. "It's cold and dreary and lifeless! It's not good enough for her!"

"I say!" a voice hailed them from the upper regions. "*Isn't* it nice to see you here! I am glad you've come! I *say*! You've got new coats! Oh, what a nice one, Jenny-Wren!" and the Pixie, four foot ten and a half, and looking very tiny, hung over the top railing to welcome them.

"Well, don't you think we need new coats?" Jen laughed. "Of all the dismal, chilly, wet, clammy places to live in, London's the worst! Why, we've been sitting out, in the abbey!"

"It isn't really. Only in March. You mustn't say rude things about London; I love it! I'm never quite happy away from town. Theobald's Row is just heavenly;" there was defiance in the Pixie's tone.

"That crowded street we've just crossed, with the buses and things? It's not exactly my idea of heaven!" Joy laughed.

"Oh, but I love a London crowd! It's different from any other crowd! Are those flowers for me? Aren't they lovely? What's this?—almond? Come and put it in water; this way!" and she hustled them through rooms and into the kitchen, without time for a glance about them.

"Oh, but I want to see!" Jen remonstrated. "I believe you've got a lovely room there. I want to see it. Can't we see everything?"

"Of course you shall! Go and put your coats off; I want to see your frocks! That's my bedroom we came through; all our rooms open out of one another. Oh, aren't these lovely?" as she arranged the daffodils in a bowl. "I shall take some, and the almond, down to Plaistow to-night; do you mind? They don't get flowers like these there. I'll say they've come straight from the country."

"There are a thousand million daffies in our orchard, under the apple-trees, so you can say it safely. You're not to give them all away, though," Joy remonstrated.

"Oh, but I'll get the good of them there. And my men will love them so!"

"If there are men in the case, of course we needn't say any more! She'll give them all away to her men!" Jen mocked, coming from the bedroom. "What's on at Plaistow? And where is it, anyway?"

"I've got the loveliest classes. You must come and see them one day, but not yet; we've only just got started. At the big Y.M.C.A. Club, you know; men and girls—such dears, all of them! And we have big parties, and enjoy ourselves no end."

"It sounds all right! I'd love to come to a party!"

"You shall. I'll ask you some day. Now come and have some tea. Oh, I like your frock, Jenny-Wren! Have that for the wedding? You're to tell me all about it. I was so sorry I couldn't come, but I had a big party in Nottingham that night. What did you want to see me about?" to Joy. "You said there was something important. Is it something Moral?" in anxious capitals. "Or only folk-dancing?"

"I'm afraid it's Moral. Do you mind?" Joy looked down at her hopefully.

"No, I'm glad. But what made you think of asking me? And what is it all about?"

"I'll tell you after tea. The wedding will be better for

tea-time. There didn't seem to be anybody else," Joy said simply. "And I do want to talk to somebody in earnest, somebody who'll tell me what to do! You see things so clearly."

"It's awfully nice of you," the Pixie said soberly, as she lifted the bowl of daffodils and led the way through the bedroom again. "Aren't they lovely?" she murmured, her eyes on the blaze of yellow.

"Oh! What a gorgeous room!" Jen stood on the threshold to gaze. "I'd *never* have believed you could find a room like that inside a house like this!"

"It's so big and square." Joy, the lover of the open air, looked round the lofty room with approval. "Nice big windows! It isn't stuffy, if it is in town!"

"And the colours!" Jen's tone was full of deepest satisfaction. "Oh, I am glad we came!"

The room was deep blue, and black, and dull blue-grey, in walls and carpet, big couch and easy-chairs; here and there was a touch of vivid flame-colour, in cushions, curtains, or china.

"It's an artist's room; I love it! Oh, we only rent it, but isn't it beautiful? I do think we're lucky! Your daffodils shall stand here. Look at that beautiful blue bowl! My Nottingham class gave me that, the dears! Wasn't it lovely of them? Now come and have tea! Choose your chairs; Jenny-Wren, pass up the hotters! The kettle's boiling."

Jen lifted a plate of hot scones from the hearth. "These? I never heard them called hotters before."

"Oh, that's Oxford! We always called them hotters. Now tell me all about the wedding! What did you all wear? Was Joan's frock pretty? She'd look lovely, of course; she couldn't help it. And he didn't get married to you by mistake?" with a twinkle of amusement at Joy. "Gracious! You did give me a shock that day, when I found I'd got two of you in my class! I've never got over it. D'you remember?"

"Remember! You wanted me to go straight out and dye my tunic green, so that you'd know us apart."

"You aren't so much alike as I thought at first;" the Pixie studied her face thoughtfully. "But you're getting more like Joan, I do believe. What have you been doing to yourself lately?"

"I've thought that too," Jen said swiftly. "She is more like Joan than she used to be! It doesn't matter now that Joan's gone, but it's as well she didn't start getting like her before, or Jack might have got tied up in them."

"He never showed any signs of it coming on, that I could see! Have another hotter," and Joy flourished the dish before the Pixie.

"But tell me all about the wedding!" the Pixie demanded hungrily, and Joy plunged into the story, and ended with a laughing account of the morning adventure in the abbey, of Madam's visit, and her amused horror at being "buried alive."

"But she just loved it!" Jen added.

"Of course she did. She'll never let you forget it, though. Has everybody had enough tea? Now, Joy, what's the trouble? It *is* nice of you to come to me about it!" and the Pixie pushed away the table with a business-like air. "Pull in your chairs to the fire! Shall I switch on the light?"

"No, firelight's cosiest," Jen took the corner of the big sofa, and retired into the background, but watched Joy's face, and then the Pixie's, continually; as the one talked, the other listened thoughtfully.

Joy sat on the fender, nursing her knee, and soberly repeated what she had said the night before. The Pixie, on a low stool before the fire, listened curiously, finding in the new thoughtfulness of Joy's face the explanation of the unexpected likeness she had just discovered.

"It's the whole question of one's attitude to money," Joy said at last. "I can give it away; that's easy enough. I've plenty; I can give away a lot, and never feel it. I do try to give sensibly, but I don't give to every old person who asks! They do ask, you know. I get shoals of begging letters."

"Of course you will. But you have to sift them. In some cases you'd do more harm than good by giving money. Your part is in taking trouble to make sure you are using the money well," the Pixie said, very definitely. "Your giving of money is too easy. *You* have to give yourself; in time, and thought, and trouble. You can do a *lot* for people, if you only will. Why don't you run a little hostel in the village?"

"That's a lovely idea!" Joy said swiftly. "I like it! Go on, Pixie! And you do think I've got to take in these two infants?"

"Of course you will. Your work is waiting for you there. The schoolgirl may not bother you very much, but the heiress is another matter. You can just be the making of that child, if you will."

"Madam said I was the last person in the world she'd chose as a fit and proper guardian for a girl!" Joy said pensively. "Isn't she brutal sometimes?"

"But she took it back afterwards!" Jen's voice came out of the darkness over the Pixie's shoulder.

The Pixie dismissed Madam and her sweeping judgments with a gesture. "She doesn't understand. You hadn't told her all this?"

"Help, no! It never came into my head!"

"Then she couldn't possibly judge. Of course, you can do it beautifully. And it's a chance to give service where it's needed; to give real personal help and trouble, the kind of thing no money can buy. Isn't that what you've been feeling?"

"Yes," Joy said slowly. "Yes, I think it is. I knew you'd be definite, and go straight to the point!"

"Oh, but you had seen it for yourself! Let me know how you get on, won't you? I shall want to hear. Now I've got to run, you know, or my classes will be waiting for me. I *am* so glad you came! It *was* nice of you!"

"Couldn't I run you along to Plaistow?" Joy asked, standing on the rug in the firelight and looking down at her. "I haven't an idea where it is, but I'd find it all right."

"No, of course not. I've just time to do it, and you couldn't find it in the dark." She switched on the lights, and Jen clapped her hands softly as a bright orange glow filled the blue room.

"What pretty shades! And I suppose it's wet and cold outside! I'd forgotten the wind and sleet. Aunty Pixie, it is so nice to have seen you at home!"

The Pixie chuckled. "Come into the kitchen for three minutes! I want to put on the potatoes for Mary's dinner, and make her a fruit salad, so that it will be all ready when she comes in tired. She's due in twenty minutes. No, you can't help. Just sit on the table and talk to me," and she peeled potatoes at the sink in the diminutive kitchen at express speed. "Now make up some of those flowers in a bundle for me, will you? My men will just love them. And get into your coats. We'll all have to run."

"Yes, or Jacky-boy will have gone to classes without us! We're hoping to give Madam a surprise."

"Oh, give her my love! And let me know how you get on with your heiress! It *was* nice of you to come to me!" was the Pixie's last word, as she hung over the top railing and called good-bye after them while they clattered down the big stone steps.

CHAPTER VIII

AN EVENING WITH JACKY-BOY

JACQUELINE, or Jacky-boy came flying out to hurl herself on them at the first sound of Eirene's horn before her door.

"How late you are, Jen! Has Joy been talking somewhere? Come on; you've only just time to change!"

"Well, that is a nasty one!" Joy said indignantly. "I'm sure I don't talk *much*!"

"Come along and get ready! Have you had tea? Come up at once, then," and she ran before them upstairs to a big bedroom. "Now tell me everything while you change! How did it go off on Wednesday?"

"We'll tell you about the wedding in bed to-night," Jen interrupted, hurling her coat and frock aside. "Give me out my gym blouse and tunic, quickly, Jack. Now tell us all about to-night. That matters more just now. Who's teaching? What are you doing?"

"First there's half an hour of swords with her—Madam. We're doing 'Earsdon,'" Jack said importantly.

"Rappers! You little swank! And we've never tried them yet! That's what comes of living in town!" Joy said enviously. "I'm dying to try rappers! I will, too, at Cheltenham next summer!"

"How do you like them, Jacky-boy?" Jen had paused in her hasty toilet. "Aren't you frightened?"

"My dear, I was terrified!" Jack said solemnly, as she tossed a blue tunic to each of them. "I never dreamt it was a rapper class! I'd got the half-hour to spare, before morris; so I thought I'd go. I didn't even know who was teaching. But suddenly Madam blew in, and said we'd do 'Earsdon.' 'Earsdon!' That miners' dance! I nearly *died*! And when we started, I was simply scared stiff! I thought my head would be cut off every minute. And she kept yelling at me because I was wrong; of *course* I was wrong, all the time! Then she'd say, 'Don't look so worried, Miss Wilmot!' Worried! I was nearly dead, panting and gasping a thousand miles behind her! I nearly threw my sword at her. Then she'd get frantic: you know her way"—the other two laughed and nodded—"and she'd shout, 'Clockwise, Miss Wilmot!'—as if I could think which was clockwise, with those things buzzing round my head! So I'd turn counter-clock, and we'd be all tied up in a knot, and she'd come flying down the room at me, and say, 'It's *you*, Jacky-boy! You're wrong every time!' and the other four wondered if I was a lunatic, and they've never called me anything but Jacky-boy since. Oh, we had great fun for the first week or two!" Jack said pensively. "Now it's better, of course. I know what I'm supposed to be doing. We do have fun sometimes! I say, are you coming up for the party next week?"

"Didn't know there was one. Oh, we can't come up once a week, Jacky-boy! Unless any important business turns up, of course."

"Well, couldn't you make some?" Jack pleaded. "Oh, couldn't you come and stop for a night or two? I'll be all alone! *Do!* Then we could go to the party together! Think what fun we'd have!"

"I'd love to go to a London party!" Jen looked at Joy wistfully.

"Well, you might spare me Jen for a night or two, if you can't come yourself!" Jack urged.

"Help! What would be the good of that? Jen needs me to look after her! What happens after swords this evening, Jacky-boy?"—neatly catching and returning the pillow Jen had hurled at her.

"Madam runs along to another hall and takes morris and country for an hour each, and I go there too, for it's revision for the exam, and I'd like to take it this summer. But that's too easy for you two; you've passed your Elementary!

You'd better stay and join in the Advanced class; you'll know a lot of the girls."

"Who's teaching?" Joy asked. "Madam can't take two sets at once! I'd rather stick to her. You always have a good time with her."

"They're doing rather thrilling dances in the Advanced class, though," Jack remarked. "I watch for a minute or two sometimes. They're doing 'Bledington' just now; I'm sure your kick-jumps need practice, Joy!"

"They do!" Joy laughed. "They're the limit for badness! But I'm out to enjoy myself to-night. I shall come with you to Madam's class."

"I shall stay and watch the Advanced lot, if it's some one new teaching them," Jen decided. "I don't say I'll join in, even if they'd have me; I'm not really up to that grade. But I do love watching classes, and whoever she is, she'll be a good teacher. They all are!"

"It's only five minutes' walk," Jack explained, as they set out. "Now come on, or we'll be late, and my set will have got another Number Three. I couldn't possibly be anything but Three, of course! We'd better run!" She led the way, and Joy and Jen raced after her through the damp, quiet streets.

CHAPTER IX

OLD FRIENDS AND NEW

In a dressing-room were girls in all stages of undress; girls changing shoes, girls changing stockings, girls changing blouses, girls one and all getting into tunics and saying their worst about the weather.

Jack, throwing greetings right and left, went to look through the inner door, unbuttoning her coat as she did so.

"She's here!" briefly, to Joy. "You two had better go and explain yourselves. We *are* late!"

"Why, it's Miss Shirley!" "Why, Joy!" "And Miss Robins, from Cheltenham!" one after another recognised the new-comers.

"I say, Shirley, this is an unexpected pleasure. Where have you dropped from?" A round-faced, jolly-looking dark girl came up, tying her girdle. "Where's Joan? Isn't she with you? And what's become of Hobart?"

"Married, both of 'em," Joy assured the plump person solemnly. "Isn't it sad? Come and explain yourself to Madam, Jenny-Wren!"

"Why, it's little Robins! Where have you all come from? I say, are you all right again, Robins?"

Jen laughed and nodded, and followed Joy. "Isn't it jolly nice to be remembered?" she murmured.

The inner door opened on a big hall, with cleared floor, a piano on the platform, a dark girl tuning a violin, and Madam, in a bright green sports coat over a blue tunic, sitting on the hot water pipes to thaw herself.

"I think we'll start. It's time. Are there any more out there?" and then Madam saw the visitors, and her eyes widened in surprise. "Hal—lo? Why, Joy? Jen? Where on earth have you come from? What do you mean by it?" in mock indignation. "You never said anything about this yesterday!"

"Oh, we didn't know! We just decided to spend a night with Jack, and so we came along."

"Have you buried anybody lately?" Madam asked accusingly, and a laugh from the fiddler showed that she had heard the story.

"Not since you. One a day is about as much as I can manage," Joy retorted. "Do you mind if we watch? Jacky-boy wants us to see how clever she is. She's swanking fearfully about having learnt rappers before either of us."

"Won't you dance? There's sure to be someone away, on a night like this. Aren't you perished?" and Madam shivered and hugged the pipes again.

"Oh, but we've never touched the things! No, thanks! We'll look on," and they subsided into a corner, and watched the evolutions of the "Earsdon" dance with keen interest.

"Now I'm going with her to have some morris!" Joy sprang up eagerly, when the sword class was over.

"I'm going to stop here," said Jen. "I love Madam too, but I like watching new people. Tell Jack to come back for me; I couldn't possibly find my way home alone."

She approached the girl who had taken command, and who, conforming to the fashion of the evening, was also sitting on the radiator, rubbing her hands and making scathing comments on the temperature to the violinist.

"Do you mind if I watch for a little while, please?"

"Oh, I mind frightfully! I think I'll turn you out," and she smiled. "Aren't you going to dance? Are you quite all right again?"

"Oh!" gasped Jen, utterly taken aback. "But you don't know me? I mean, I've never been in your class? And you haven't seen me since last August, anyway; nine months! How can you remember?"

"If you will distinguish yourself, as you did, and upset the whole school on the last morning, of course you must expect to be remembered," was the retort.

Jen retired to her corner stunned, and watched the first dance still in a state of incredulous amazement, which increased when the teacher turned to her to say, "Don't you want to dance, Miss Robins? There's room in that back set."

"She even knows my name!" marvelled Jen's mind, while she explained limply that she had never learned "Bledington Trunkles."

"I loathe 'Bledington'!" a tall girl collapsed on a chair near Jen, at the end of the dance. "I shall never do kick-jumps, I'm sure of that!"

"Did anyone say it was a cold night?" another laughed. "Aren't there any more windows we could open?"

Then they were called to make four lines for a 'Bledington' jig, to show what progress the difficult step had made, and all sprang eagerly to their places, heat, exhaustion, everything forgotten.

Jen in her corner had been unnoticed. They were all absorbed in the enjoyment of the moment. She watched the teaching with deep interest, her eyes going continually from the class to the teacher.

"She's interesting, isn't she?" and at the end of the dance someone sat down rather breathlessly beside Jen; she had b en watching her absorbed face, and now spoke sympathetically.

"Awfully!" Jen turned quickly. "Oh, weren't you at Cheltenham?"

"Yes. I knew you by sight. I'm afraid I'm bad at names. I was in Room C with you the first week."

"Oh, then you know Madam and the Pixie!" Jen said joyfully. "Don't you write girls' books?"

"Well, I do. And I do know Madam and the Pixie. Are you quite well again?"

"Everybody knows all about me!" Jen said, in a tone of mournful satisfaction. "Quite, thanks. Isn't it thrilling?—writing books, I mean?"

"It's very interesting!" the Writing Person said sedately.

"So are people! I was frightfully interested in all your crowd at Cheltenham! You look quite all right again!"

"Oh, I am! I could do morris jigs, if I happened to know them! But the less said about my kick-jumps the better, and I'm quite aware of it. I have tried them, but that's all."

"Oh, they're brutes! But you can't have 'Bledington' without them, and 'Bledington' as a whole is too good to live without, so the kick-jumps have to be thrown in somehow."

"You're frightfully keen on the dances, aren't you?" Jen asked, with interest.

"I'm frightfully interested! Last term we did the 'Longborough' dances; they were all new to me, and I was a bit scared of them at first, but it's gorgeous to feel I understand them at last! I could hardly restrain myself when I found we were really going to do 'Princess Royal' to that wonderful tune. I wanted to get up and cheer."

Jen laughed. "Well, why didn't you?"

"Now she's going to make us have another go at 'Lumps.' Won't you come and try it?"

Jen shook her head and laughed. "No, thanks! I'll watch you instead."

"I'd very strongly advise you to watch some one else! I only play at it, I'm afraid," and the Writing Person went to take her place.

"I'm glad I stayed to watch," Jen said, at the end. "It's better fun than dancing."

"It's as good, anyway. And not half so hot!" her new friend conceded, sitting down again rather breathlessly.

"Do you come every Friday?" Jen asked with interest.

"I wouldn't miss a Friday for any money!" the Writing Person said fervently. "My work would simply stop. I couldn't carry on without Fridays to buck me up to it."

"How funny! Oh, here she comes! She must be after you. What have you been doing?"

It was Jen who was wanted, however. "Come along,

Miss Robins! You've embraced that radiator long enough. Haven't you the courage to join in 'Chelsea Reach'?"

"May I? I'd simply love it!" and Jen laughed and sprang up, throwing off her coat.

"I danced the whole hour of Country!" Jen informed the rest, as they sat down starving to supper. "They do have super teachers! And they're doing wonderful new dances in that grade. We had a gorgeous thing called 'Spring Garden'; I'd never even heard of it, but wasn't it appropriate for March?

"We had the usual kind of jolly old time you always do have when Madam's in charge, and all enjoyed ourselves no end," said Joy. "I don't know how she does it, but she does make you love it! I think it's because you can see she's having such a good time herself. She's frightfully infectious, of course."

"Sounds nasty," Jack remarked. "She's tremendously alive, anyway."

"*I* had a perfectly gorgeous evening!" Jen said loftily.

CHAPTER X

THE HEIRESS IN THE PULPIT

"Now we've got to face our problems!" said Joy, as they sped westwards next morning. "You're very quiet, Jenny-Wren! What's the matter? Did you dance too much last night? Too much 'Spring Garden'?"

"No, but I'm having a big think about last night. I'll tell you later, Wild Cat," and Jen sat in absorbed thought as Eirene left the Uxbridge rivers and bridges behind, and sped towards the commons and wide roads of Beaconsfield.

At the gates of the big day-school in Wycombe, Joy paused to leave a note, written the night before, assuring her old headmistress she would be delighted to welcome Rosamund as soon as convenient.

"You aren't going in?"

"No, I want to get home, and square things with Ann and Maidlin. If the infant really doesn't want to come, we may have a breezy time, considering the Italian temper!"

"Perhaps she'll have run away again!"

"Not if she only did it because she didn't want to come to the Hall!" Joy said swiftly.

"As if there could be a nicer family than you and me! I do wonder whether she really wants to come or not!" Jen pondered. "It's obvious she didn't want to be shoved at you, but then nobody would. I'd like to know how she really feels."

"So would I. But I don't suppose we ever shall."

As soon as lunch was over, and Joy had changed, she slipped on her coat and went bareheaded through the garden to the abbey, to have her talk with Ann. Although it was Saturday afternoon, there were no tourists in the abbey, the bitter March wind being distinctly discouraging for country rambles.

She found the caretaker sitting over the fire in her little front room. Maidlin was nowhere to be seen.

"Oh, Ann!" Joy plunged into business at once, "I just blew in—literally! I was blown right across the garth!—to say I think it will be best if your Maidlin comes to us, after all. If I find I'm not making a good job of it, I'll find some better place. But at present it seems simpler for her just to come to us."

Ann had risen, and was clasping her hands in nervous excitement. "Oh, Miss Joy? Do you mean it, really? I'd rather the child went to you than to anybody in the whole world!"

"Oh, Ann, dear, don't be an idiot!" Joy said brusquely. "There are thousands of better places for her, and I'm a very bad person to look after her. But I do happen to be on the spot. Will she be willing to come, by the way?"

"She's in the abbey, Miss Joy. She's there whenever she can slip away from me."

"I'll find her and have a talk with her. Now, Ann, since she's out, we'll talk business for a few minutes! What about money? She'll want clothes and things. Shall I advance it, till her father comes home?"

"There's the gentleman in London, Miss Joy. 'Twere in the letter, that he'd give us all the money we needed for her."

"I remember; a lawyer. Give me the address, and I'll write to him and explain the arrangements we're making. I think I'll take Maidlin up to see him, and to do some shopping. I shan't send her to school at present," Joy spoke as if she had suddenly become the mother of a schoolgirl daughter, which indeed was how she felt. "Now I'll go and find her. Do you know at all where she'll be?"

"She—she climbs up to the pulpit, Miss Joy," Ann faltered. "I've told her she didn't ought to, but she don't do no harm, so she says."

"She fell out of it, almost on to my head, two days ago," Joy laughed.

Deliberately, she climbed up the little steps to the reader's pulpit, and confronted the defiant eyes of the small girl curled up there with a book. "Is there room for two? Will you let me in? Have you decided this is the nicest spot in the whole abbey?"

Maidlin's eyes fell before hers, in confused remembrance of that last meeting out in the road. "The refectory's the best, and you can see it all from here."

"Have you been along the secret passage to the Hall? But I suppose not. Ann would only show you the beginning of it."

"She wouldn't let me go. She said the door at the other end was shut. And I hadn't a torch."

"Or you'd have gone without her? But it has to be kept shut, you know. We can't have people wandering about inside our walls while we're living there. But I can open it with my key. Suppose you come back through the tunnel, and have tea with me? You're going to live with me, aren't you?"

"No!" burst explosively from Maidlin, and she sprang up, ready for another wild flight.

But Joy barred her way. "If you push past me, I shall fall off the steps and break my neck, or sprain my ankle! That would be rather an unkind way of refusing an invitation; don't you think so? Why don't you want to come? The house seems so empty without Joan; and Jen isn't going to stay with me very long. Make room for me up there, and we'll talk about it. Why don't you want to come?"

The child's head was bent, her long black hair hiding her face. Her shoulders shook. "Aunty asked you to ask me! You had to do it! You feel you've got to have me! It—it isn't fair!"

For a moment Joy longed wildly for Joan. Then she pulled herself together, and spoke seriously, though very gently. "It's difficult to know what to say! I'm afraid I'm not very clever. It's difficult for me to make you believe I'm in earnest. I said I'd rather not, because I didn't feel good enough. Perhaps," unkindly, "that's how you feel, too? Of course, if that's so——"

"Oh!" It was jerked out of Maidlin by her indignant surprise. "I'd *love* to come!" she panted. "It's only—only——"

Joy's eyes gleamed. But she only said quietly, "I thought you hated the very idea, and I supposed perhaps I wasn't good enough, for some reason. Don't let's have any more nonsense about it! I've thought it over, and I really want you to come. I'll do the best I can for you; but *don't* go and make me feel I'm not good enough! Unless you really think so, of course. I'd rather know the worst."

Maidlin was shaking with passionate sobbing. "I'd rather have you than anybody in the world, Miss Joy! But—but I thought you didn't—you couldn't really——"

"I guess that's good enough!" Joy said quietly. "Now, never let me hear you say *Miss* Joy again! It will hurt my feelings dreadfully. If we quarrel, you may say it, but not till then, unless you're trying to have a fight with me. See? Now, say, 'Yes, Joy dear, I quite understand!' like a good kid."

Maidlin looked at her, growing red, then white. Then a spark lit in her dark eyes. "I quite understand, *Joy dear*! But I—I think it would be rather fun to have a fight with you! Are you—are you nice when you fight?" rather breathlessly.

"I'm perfectly dreadful," Joy assured her solemnly. "But I'll pillow-fight you to-night, if you like. Now come away home through the secret passage. Aunty and Jen are expecting us to tea. I want to tell you all my plans for you; some of them are quite thrilling! I've been thinking about you all the way home from town this morning. Don't you want to hear all about it? Oh, are you shy?"

"I won't know—what to say," Maidlin hung back.

"How funny it must feel to be shy, and funnier still not to know what to say!" Joy said reflectively. "Now, Maidlin, my child, it may feel funny, but you'll find it very inconvenient, so the sooner you get out of it the better. Just come and have tea with us, and listen! I believe I talk quite a lot; I'm always being told so! I know Jen and I yatter and babble for hours at a time, and all about nothing. I'll get a torch from Ann, and we'll go by the tunnel. You'd like to see it, wouldn't you?"

"A torch, please, Ann! Maidlin's coming to tea with me. Thanks! Come on, kid!" and Joy returned to Maidlin, who had hung behind in the cloisters, leaving Ann breathless but delighted.

"Race me to the old door!" Joy commanded, and broke into a run. "Now go carefully down the steps! Don't fall over the edge! And now follow me. This is my private Underground Railway! All stations to Mansion House! Change for West Ham and Barking! First turning on the right for Abinger Hall and tea!"

CHAPTER XI

JEN'S " THINK "

"THIS," said Joy indignantly, "was *not* a part of the entertainment I had planned for you, Madalena! The beastly thing's bolted on the inside, and we're stuck."

They were still in the secret tunnel, but had climbed the steps and made their way along the passage which ran inside the wall of the big entrance-hall of the house, the door at the top of the inner stair having yielded at once to Joy's key. The panel-door was less obliging, however. She had unlocked it with the key which hung on a ring with the key of the abbey gate; but to her dismay the door still would not open. She pushed and shook, then gave it up.

"Just yell 'Help!' when I do, kid! We've got to make somebody hear us. Jen has evidently gone upstairs."

Maidlin got to business promptly, and they both shouted and hammered on the door to such good purpose that presently it was thrown open, and Jen stood eyeing them severely.

"Not at home to-day! No hawkers, canvassers, or circulars allowed! Oh, Wild Cat, what a lunatic you are! You bolted it yourself! You know you did, because of the wedding presents!"

"I know. I haven't a word to say. I forgot," Joy said limply. "Come and wash, Madalena! If you're as dirty as I am, after thumping on that door for ten minutes, you'll be glad to."

Maidlin was very quiet during the hour that followed, but her dark eyes were very busy, taking in everything—the beautiful staircases and bathrooms, the glimpses of big rooms as she passed, the long corridors, the pretty bedroom, next to Jen's, which had been prepared for her. She was still quiet, but still very busy, during the homely tea in a corner of the big lounge hall, when, with Joy and Jen and Mrs. Shirley, she sat by the blazing fire on the big open hearth. She answered Mrs. Shirley's kind remarks shyly, was very careful not to drop crumbs, and listened in breathless interest and surprise to the stream of chaff and chatter between Joy and Jen.

Then the tea tray was carried away, the tables disappeared, Mrs. Shirley went upstairs again, and the three girls drew the curtains, made up the fire, and sat in its light to talk.

"I've a gorgeous plan for next week!" said Joy. "Maidlin ought to go and see her lawyer—it's all right, infant! Don't look so scared! I'll do the talking. But he ought to see you do really exist—And she'd like to do some shopping. We'll go up in Eirene on Thursday, do business all day, and run along to Jack's after tea. You know how she begged and prayed this morning that we'd come for the party! Jacky-boy is Jen's chum, Maidlin; and she lives in town, and we spent last night with her, and she loved having us. But her dad and mother have to go away for a few days next week, and she's just dying to have us to keep her company. We'll *all* go to the party, Jenny-Wren! Maidlin will love to see it. How's that?"

"Oh!" Jen gave a little shriek of joy. "I've been dying to go to one for years! Months, anyway! I'll get some good out of being a member at last. Tell me who'll be there?"

"Everybody who counts for anything at all will be there; Madam, and her man, and all that lot, and, of course, the Prophet and his Little Page. And we'll dance country-dances for two hours; and the Director will play for us himself. And you know that's worth living for!"

"I can't wait till Thursday!" Jen sighed happily.

"And on Friday we'll see. Perhaps we could take the Pixie out to lunch, or go to call on Madam. I'll do some ringing up, and see what everybody's plans are. We'll show Maidlin a little of London, and see how she likes Eirene."

"But I can't go seeing all your friends!" Maidlin faltered, aghast.

"Why not? You're lucky to have the chance. They're nice sort of friends to have!" Joy said. "You'll like Jacky-boy; she's just a kid, anyway. As for the party, nobody will take any notice of you! They'll all be far too busy enjoying themselves. You'll just sit in a corner and watch. They're all folk-dancers; and that means they're ordinary jolly natural people, who love to have a good time. Jenny-Wren, isn't it so?"

Jen had been staring into the fire in absorbed silence, but woke with a start. "Rather! That's part of the big think I had in the car this morning."

"And now you're going to tell us all about it!" Joy commanded. "I want to know what kept you so quiet for such ages! Most unnatural, it was!"

"I was thinking about last night—the whole of it. The sleet, and the wind, and the wet, cold streets, and that dark tunnel entry; then all the jolly crowd of girls inside, forgetting all about the weather and their work and worries, and just giving themselves up to the old music and those wonderful dances. To heaps of those girls, who work really hard all day, in one way or another, those evening classes once a week must be something to live for, something they'll count up the days for, a kind of oasis in a desert. Wouldn't you live for your morris and country classes at night, and nearly die when they were over for another week? Some of them are in offices. The Writing Person told me; she knows a lot of them. One lives near Oxford Circus—a tomboy-looking girl with bobbed curly hair, and a dinky little frock instead of a tunic; made it herself, too! Goes camping in a real proper tent in August, and comes to the Summer Schools for dancing; prefers it to any other kind of holiday, though she doesn't get very long. She *lives* near Oxford Circus, and works in an office all day, and simply has to fly to get to the Friday classes! Has to do all the work of looking after her room, and dressmaking, and so on, after she gets home at night. Well, don't you think the dancing means a good lot to a girl like that?"

Jen paused for breath. Maidlin was listening in rapt interest, her wide eyes showing how new such talk was to her.

Joy said urgently, "Go on! But how did you find out so much about the girls, all in one evening? Oh, was it that Writing Person?"

"I asked her about them, in between dances. Most of the girls are teachers, and want their certificates because they could get better posts if they had them. Well, fancy if you'd taught a class of sixty small infants every day for a week! Think how you'd feel by Friday night!"

"I can't!" Joy said again. "I'd be dead!"

"Some of them love it, of course, and feel it's the only work in the world worth doing. But even if you love it, you must get very tired. When they're just about done in, at the end of the week, they come along and dance; and they're bullied themselves, instead of having to worry about bullying their infants; and don't you think it's a *rest*? Even if it nearly kills them with hard work, it's a rest! The Writing Person says they once did nine country dances in an hour, and she could hardly lie still in bed after it, because she was so sore! She's writing all the time, and nothing she's ever found yet helps her to keep fresh so well as folk-dancing does. She says time after time she's worked all day, till she felt just empty, like a balloon without any air in it—writing, or typing, or correcting proofs; and then, when she's felt only ready for bed, but really too fagged to sleep, she's made herself go to dancing instead, and done an hour or two; and she's gone home far less tired than she went out. Then she's slept well, and done stacks of work next day. She always works best the day after classes."

"I expect it stirs her all up, and so she gets new ideas," Joy said shrewdly.

"Well, Madam and all those people are helping her, just as they help the teachers and the office people! I think they're doing a *big* thing for girls who have to work, by giving them folk-dancing in the evenings, to keep them fresh and help them to carry on. That's what my 'think' was, Joy; what a big thing those London classes are for London girls! Is there one before the party on Thursday? For if so, I'm going to watch, or to join in, if they'll let me!"

"Sword, morris, and country! We'll take Maidlin; she'll love it. I wonder who'll be teaching, though?"

"You can't have Madam all the time!" Jen laughed. "I don't mind who's teaching! Play us something, Joy! Maidlin ought to hear your piano."

"What do you want?" Joy went to open her treasure.

"Something of your own. I heard you trying over something after lunch. Had you got a new idea?"

"'Tisn't nearly ready yet; it's only scrappy," but Joy began to play wandering chords, and then drifted into a swaying melody.

Joy wandered into another of her dreams, and from that to another, with now and then a glance at Maidlin's enthralled face in the firelight glow. Presently, however, she broke into a swinging chanty tune and Maidlin jumped with surprise as Jen, laughing joyfully, took up the words,—

"I think I heard the old man say,
O you Rio!
I think I heard the old man say,
We're bound for Rio Grande!"

And while Maidlin listened in growing surprise and delight, Joy played on and on, and her voice and Jen's rang out and filled the room, in ballad, and carol, and shanty, but most of all in folk-songs of the countryside.

"She's fond of music!" Joy murmured once, as she turned

the pages. "She's sure to have inherited a voice along with the fortune and the temper and the name! Goes with the black hair and eyes! She's probably shy; she would be with us, anyway. But she likes music, and that's a big thing."

"She'll love Thursday evening in town!" Jen said, with conviction.

CHAPTER XII

JOY'S TWINS

MAIDLIN, in a prettier bedroom than she had ever dreamed of, sat up in bed and listened to the laughter and chattering from the next room. Joy and Jen had gone to bed early, as soon, indeed, as they had seen their guest safely in her room. But "going to bed" did not mean settling down for the night, in Joy's house, it appeared. Maidlin had heard light footsteps pass her door, and now judged from the sounds she heard that Joy was sitting on Jen's bed. She listened wistfully, and felt lonely.

It was nearly an hour before she heard Jen's door open and close again, very softly; and then her own was opened, almost without a sound, and Joy, in her dressing-gown and long heavy plait, crept up to see if she were asleep.

"Why, Maidlin!" she whispered. "What's the matter? You aren't homesick, are you? Were we keeping you awake? I am sorry! We tried to whisper, but I'm afraid we kept forgetting. We always pow-wow at bedtime. Is there anything you'd like?"

Maidlin had been sitting up waiting, but had crouched suddenly at her approach, her face hidden in her pillow. "I wanted you," the words were stifled. "I wanted to tell you something. I don't feel honest. But I couldn't say it while anybody was there."

Once more Joy had that wild desire for Joan, that sense

of unfitness for a crisis. "What's wrong?" she asked gently, sitting on the bed.

"You thought I didn't want to come!" Maidlin panted. "I was *dying* to come, all the time! I'd heard about you and I'd watched for you in the abbey. I was watching you on the garth in the morning, before that lady came. I'd seen you dance there; and I'd heard you sing. And then aunty said she'd *ask* you to have me, *ask* you to take me to *live* with you, in your beautiful house; and I knew you'd feel it was awful cheek, and you couldn't help hating me; and—and I nearly died. I felt better when you said no. And then you came suddenly, when I couldn't get away, and somehow you made me believe it was all right, and I could come, and you wouldn't mind having me. And the whole world seemed too wonderful to be true. But—but you know how it is at night! I thought it must be all a mistake. And I thought I'd tell you how I'd felt, and how I'd wanted to come more more than anything I could think of."

It was very difficult to know what to say.

"And is that all?" Joy asked presently.

Maidlin quivered again. "What more can there be? You *can't* want me really!"

"I think there's something else, and you're fighting against it, because you won't quite let yourself believe it. You've said a lot; but have you said it all?"

"To-night!" Maidlin whispered, gaining courage, "you—you made me feel as if I'd come home and you were glad to have me. But it couldn't be true!"

"Right-o!" Joy said happily. "Then all's well. If you've only got a fit of the nerves because it's nearly midnight, then I needn't worry! I thought for a few minutes I'd made you feel I didn't want you; and I was going to feel really *bad*! Silly!" her voice was caressing, in spite of its reproof. "Things are bound to feel queer the first night. That's why I came to see if you were all right. Now are you going to sleep, without worrying about anything more at all?"

"There isn't anything left to worry about," Maidlin whispered fervently. "I didn't know even you could be so kind!"

Joy laughed, but gently, and kissed her and laid her down. "Poor soul! You have had a day of it."

Before breakfast, in the bare apple orchard Joy found Jen gathering wild daffodils for the house, well wrapped up in furs, but revelling in the sun which tempered the keen wind. The Hall and the abbey, lying at the foot of the hills, were sheltered from east winds, and as soon as the sun shone spring came back.

"Where's Maidlin? Haven't you brought her out? Isn't it just great, this morning? I knew, the moment I woke, that I'd got to pick daffodils!" Jen's voice rang out in greeting.

"Maidlin's sleeping the sleep of the very-much-tired-out-infant. So I told them not to wake her, even for brekker. You see, Jenny-Wren, we had a bit of a pow-wow last night, after I'd said good-night to you," Joy said soberly.

"Oh?" Jen looked up quickly from her golden sheaf. "What, with Maidlin? At that time of night? *Joy*!"

"I know. Wasn't it awful? But the kid was sitting up waiting for me. She had to get it off her chest. I want to tell you about it," and as they went towards the house, Joy repeated the conversation, her face very serious.

"How nice of her!" was Jen's only comment, but she looked sober too. "I say, Joy, it's a big responsibility, to have someone who feels things so deeply!"

"I want to talk it over with Aunty Pixie again! I feel as if we'd moved on several steps since we saw her. But, so far as I've gone all by myself, I've come to this—just to let Maidlin live with us and be one of the family and get used to our ways. In time, of course, she'll have to go to school, but her father may come home and arrange that. I want first of all to help her to feel at home with us. D'you think that's all right?"

"It sounds quite all right," Jen said thoughtfully. "She's

not half so bad as she might be, you know, Joy. She's been well taught. There's nothing wrong with her."

"I want to see the other aunt. She must have taught Maidlin very carefully, always remembering that her father might want her some day. No, she hasn't much to unlearn. She only has to get used to us, and that will soon come. She's been to good schools; I asked a few questions. The only thing I'd really like to start her on at once would be French conversation. For her, that really is important. But I can't talk French, and you can't talk French, so there we are! I'm beginning to wonder what there is I can do! Do mothers always feel what useless creatures they are?"

"Mothers!" Jen laughed. "Is she adopted, then? You were only her guardian yesterday!"

"I felt like her mother last night."

"I say, Joy, what about the other girl—Miss Macey's kid?" cried Jen.

"What about her? She'll come after school to-morrow. I think I'll fetch her in Eirene."

"How much are you going to tell her about Maidlin?"

"I've been thinking about that. There are only two ways; to tell her the whole thing, or just to say Maidlin's here on a visit."

"Yes. Well, wouldn't that be wiser? Suppose she's snobby, and isn't nice to her? Maidlin will know in a minute. She's evidently very quick at feeling things. It would upset her, wouldn't it?"

"Hideously! It would be easier to know what to do if I knew Rosamund even a little. Schoolgirls are so different! I'm inclined to tell Rosamund the whole story and risk it, Jenny-Wren," they were standing by the sundial on the lawn. "We'll hope she's got some sense. Probably she'll be thrilled with excitement at living with so romantic a heroine as an heiress to an Italian fortune! I know I should have been, at her age."

Jen laughed. "We'll hope so. I say, Joy, we'll have some dancing! There will be four of us. We'll teach Maidlin

'Hey, Boys' on the cloister garth, as Joan taught me. We could do all the squares for four. It would be awfully good for the kid! We'll see if she's fascinated by Thursday night!"

"I'm game. But I'm not game for secrets. I hate them. I shall have a talk with Rosamund, and tell her all about it. She can help Maidlin a lot, if she will."

"I do wonder what kind of kid she is!" Jen said thoughtfully, as they went towards the house. "It will make a lot of difference to everybody!"

"I wish she wasn't coming," Joy said frankly. "One at a time would have been quite enough for me! I really would rather *not* have had twins!"

"It is a handful for you, you poor dear!" Jen laughed sympathetically. "I'll do anything I can to help!"

"I know you will, and I'm glad you're here. But when all's said and done, they're my twins, and I've got to see the job through," Joy said mournfully.

CHAPTER XIII

THE UNKNOWN QUANTITY

"You are lucky, Rosamund!" Barbara, the Queen of the previous May Day ceremony, paused enviously at the big gates, as she wheeled out her cycle.

"I know," Rosamund said.

"If Jen Robins is still there, give her my love," said Nesta.

"Is she nice? I've only seen her in the distance. She didn't come for Babs's crowning, last May!"

"Oh, awfully jolly, and always good fun! I wish we were all going with you! We did once, you know; the whole school, in the dip. time. And we lived in the Hall; it's a gorgeous old house!"

"I've never seen it, or the abbey. But I've heard heaps about them. And I've seen Joy at Club evenings. She looks awfully good fun, too," Rosamund's eyes were on the Risborough road. "She's fetching me in her car. Isn't it super of her?"

Then with a warning toot, Eirene swept down on them from the other direction, making them all jump.

Joy, wearing her suit and no hat, jumped out. "Which is Rosamund? Right-o kid! Pitch your things in behind, and get in beside me. I'll just run in and speak to Miss Macey. Hallo, Babs! How are Mirry and the baby? You all right, Nesta? Give my love to Peg and Edna, Moll!"

Her eyes had cast a quick, anxious glance over her new "twin," but it was not easy to tell much from a mere look. Rosamund was tall for her age, and pale, and looked as if life in town had not suited her. But her eyes were very bright and her face eager, and she did not look shy. She wore the school hat and regulation blue tunic and green girdle, under a warm blue coat, and her hair hung to her waist in two yellow plaits.

She was in the car, with all her belongings, by the time Joy came striding out, and the envious friends, reinforced by several more, were waiting to see her off. They shouted their farewells as Eirene crept away; then the car gathered speed and raced along the High Street, and the girls turned regretfully to go on their own much less exciting homeward ways.

Rosamund turned to Joy, before they had rounded the first corner. "It's awfully decent of you to have me!" she said warmly. "I will try not to be a trouble to you. But—I must say it! It is simply gorgeous to think of living with you at the abbey!"

Joy laughed. "You may not think it's so gorgeous when you have all this ride on very hot days, or in pouring rain! Where's your bike?"

"Miss Macey said I'd better come by train to-morrow and

ride home, as you wouldn't want to take the bike in the car."

"I'd have squeezed it in. Mind you're up early, then, or you won't catch the train. You won't want to do that often; it's too roundabout. You have to change at Risborough, you know; an awful nuisance. Look here! I've something to tell you," Joy said abruptly, as they left the town behind and began to climb the road to the hills.

"I've been all over the town, seeing if I could pick up anything decent for a girl. We're going shopping in London on Thursday, but I wanted to get her something to go in. I want to tell you about her."

Rosamund's face was alight with interest as she waited eagerly. "I love stories! The girls say the abbey is full of them, and that they're always happening to *you*!"

Joy laughed. "We've had our share. Now listen very carefully!" and Joy began on the story she had told to Madam in the crypt, with its later developments, leaving out nothing but the fact that Maidlin's coming to the Hall had been suggested by her aunt.

"Now you understand the situation! You're going to drop into the middle of it, and I'm counting on you to be sporting enough to give Jen and me some help, and not make things harder for us," Joy said frankly.

Rosamund had been looking grave. But now her face lit up. "I'd simply love to help! What is there I can do? How old is the heiress? What do you call her?"

"Maidlin—Madalena. Fourteen. She's not uneducated, or anything like that. But she's shy and awkward, and feels everything fearfully strange. I want you to be nice to her, that's all, and to behave as if it was the most natural thing in the world for girls to come into Italian fortunes! Maidlin's shy, as I've said; she doesn't feel any too much at home with us yet. Now you aren't shy! I saw that in two secs. You'll shake down and be at home in no time, long before she will, if she's left to herself. Can't you just be friendly with her, as you would be with any other girl who happened to be visiting in the same house? If you'll do that, you'll really help me and Jen, and we'll be glad you're there."

Rosamund's eyes were alight. Joy had done wisely in appealing to her for help. "I'll do any mortal thing I can! I'll be fearfully bucked if I can really help. How does Maidlin feel about my coming?"

"Feel? I don't know. I just told her. How do you mean?" It had not occurred to Joy that there could be any difficulty here.

"I thought she might feel I was a nuisance, coming butting in."

"Oh, that would be too silly! 'Tisn't any business of hers whom I choose to ask."

But Rosamund was nearer Maidlin's age, and in some ways more able to understand her point of view. "I hope she won't loathe me, that's all—Oh!" as they came to the edge of the hills and saw all the view of the vale of Aylesbury spread below them. "Oh! How perfectly gorgeous! Do we go down there?"

Joy laughed. "That's something like what Jen said when she got to this very spot for the first time. She was on the step of my bike. Yes, we go down," and they took the winding road carefully.

"It is ripping of you to let me come here!" Rosamund breathed, when she saw the Hall. "Oh, what a lovely house!"

"That's why!" Joy said bluntly. "Why I let you come; and Maidlin. I'd be a pig if I kept it all to myself. Yes, I thought that would bring Jen out!" as in answer to the blast of the horn Jen appeared in the big doorway. "Where's Maidlin, Jenny-Wren? This is Rosamund!"

"Glad to see you!" Jen said hospitably. "How's everybody down at school? Seen any of my crowd lately? Nesta or Molly, or any of that lot?"

"They saw me off. They all sent their love, and said, when are you coming to see them? They say they haven't seen you since the Hamlet dance at Christmas, except in the distance at weddings," Rosamund laughed.

"Sounds as if I spent all my time attending weddings!"

"Well, you do, rather!" Joy jeered. "You only come to see us when we provide a wedding for you and let you be a bridesmaid! You'll have to take the chief part in the next, though. I'm never going to have one. So perhaps we'll get a rest from weddings. Where's Maidlin?"

"She ran away when she heard the horn." Jen looked troubled. "I suppose she's upstairs. She's been awfully queer all afternoon, Joy. I don't know what was making her so grumpy."

"Me, I expect," Rosamund said grimly. "I rather thought she wouldn't be frightfully pleased to hear I was coming. What do we do now?" and the eyes of all three girls met in dismay.

"Smack her!" Joy burst out explosively. "Gracious me! I'll talk to her, silly child."

Jen caught her arm. "No, Joy, don't! You'll make fearful trouble; you'll ruin everything! I say, come inside. If she's in her room, she'll hear us talking, and that won't help. Don't you *see*? It's because she's so crazy about you. She can't bear to think of sharing you with anybody. Then to-day, before she's had time to get used to it, and—and find her balance, so to speak—you coolly inform her there's another girl coming! Now, I ask you, could you expect a kid who feels things deeply to take it calmly?"

Joy, standing before the fire, was pulling off her big gloves, her head bent. "Yes, I think so!" she said defiantly at last. "I see what you mean, Jen, and how you think she felt. But I do think she's to blame. I still don't see that she had any right to expect to monopolise the house and —and me! She's got to see she's wrong, and she's got to be nice to Rosamund."

"I'm awfully sorry about it!" Rosamund began, but Jen interrupted.

"I don't say Maidlin's right. I know she isn't. But I do

understand how she feels. Joy, what right have you to expect Maidlin to be perfect at fourteen?"

"I don't. But jealousy's a horrid, catty thing. Oh!" Joy sighed. "Why did I ever take on this job? To let the kid live here was all right, but to bring her up properly is quite another thing!"

"Wouldn't it be better to take no notice, if we can? Tea's ready; shan't I go up and tell her, and pretend there's nothing wrong?"

"Well, if you think it will work," Joy tossed her cap on to the settle. "I'm sure Rosamund's dying for her tea. I say, I'm most awfully sorry about all this!" and she turned impulsively to the schoolgirl.

"I'm just awfully sorry I've upset her," Rosamund said anxiously. "I feel as if you ought to send me back to school."

"Not for half a second! I wouldn't give in to her for the world! What's up, Jen? Isn't she there?"

Jen had come flying down again. "She isn't in her room, nor with Mrs. Shirley. Where can she have gone, Joy? Out into the garden?"

"Tea is once more postponed!" Joy said dramatically. "With an explosive article like an Italian heiress, you never know where you are. Oh, help! How trying it is to be a mother! Especially to such an unknown quantity as an Italian temper!" she sighed, as the search-parties scattered in various directions.

CHAPTER XIV

THE WISDOM OF JENNY-WREN

"SHE couldn't have thought of the tunnel, surely!" Joy murmured, her search of the attics having proved fruitless. She sped downstairs, and found the panel door unbolted, as she had half expected. "The monkey! She must have noticed I'd never locked it after coming home by Underground on Saturday! Here, Jen! Rosamund! You haven't found her? No; well, I believe she's gone down the secret passage."

"It's awfully decent of her to give me a chance of seeing it so soon!" Rosamund said joyfully, as, full of excitement, she followed Joy by the light of the torch.

"There is that way to look at it, of course! I thought you'd be mad with her because she'd done you out of your tea."

"Oh, what's tea, compared with secret passages?" Rosamund laughed delightedly. "I say! Fancy living in a house with walls so thick that we can walk inside them! Aren't you afraid of burglars?"

"The door's bolted on our side, just in case anyone got into the abbey, though I don't see how they could do it," Joy was holding the torch low and searching every corner. "The little monkey can't have gone far without a light, and she had no time to get one."

"Don't fall over her, then," Jen was just behind them.

"Well, Madalena, I do think you're unkind!" Joy had stopped suddenly at the door at the end of the passage. Beyond it were the steps leading down into the real tunnel. Maidlin, in a miserable heap, was crouched against the door. "I'd locked this door, had I?" Joy said, with satisfaction. "I'm glad I remembered to do one thing properly, anyway!

Well, infant, what kind of game do you call this to play with us? Hide and seek's a very good game, but you're awfully inconsiderate in the time you choose for it! Now would you really rather stay here, or are you coming back to tea?"

"Oh, couldn't we explore the passage?" Rosamund begged. "We've only just started!"

"No, my child, you could not! You shall, of course; but not to-night. Maidlin can take you through, all the way to the abbey, some day, and tell you all about it. But at this moment there's tea, tea, and nothing but tea. Come on, you two! My inner man is demanding hot scones and cakes."

Maidlin, breathless and half-sobbing still, saw them go, saw the light grow fainter. In desperation she started up and ran after them.

Jen was bringing up the rear. She felt a shy touch on her arm, and, without turning, she drew the trembling hand into hers, making no comment. Maidlin, subdued enough now, went in bewildered silence, sure only of one thing, that she did not understand these strange new people. She had not been scolded; she had not been stormed at, nor reproached. Maidlin, utterly bewildered, began to wonder if she had been silly.

When they reached the big hall, Joy's only comment was, "Tea will be poured out in three minutes, but only those who have washed their hands *and faces* will get any. Maidlin, you might show Rosamund the bathroom. Miss Robins, you and I, being no longer children, will retire to our own rooms to attend to our toilet!"

A shout of derisive laughter from Rosamund greeted this remark. Maidlin, in increasing bewilderment, stared from one to the other.

"Oh, that was a *very* feeble joke!" Joy said crushingly. "I can do *much* better than that! Glad to have amused you, all the same, children. Come on, Miss Robins, *do*!"

"Where is the bathroom? I'm dying for some tea!" Rosamund turned to staring Maidlin. "Is Miss Shirley always like that? The girls said she was a frightful sport," she remarked, as they washed. She had taken her cue from Joy, and no one could have guessed from her casual tone that any awkward feeling lay between them.

"I don't understand her, half the time," Maidlin's tone was dangerously shaky.

"Oh, well! You just laugh, when she's kidding."

"But how do you know?"

"When she's pulling your leg? Oh, you just know."

"I don't. I don't know what she means, half the time. My aunty never talked like that."

"No, I don't suppose she did!" Rosamund said to herself. To Maidlin she said lightly, "I'll wink at you when it's all utter rot they're talking, and then you'll know. Think I ought to do my hair again? Oh, I guess I'll make it do! Why don't you plait yours? I'll plait it for you to-morrow, shall I? I love doing people's hair. Have you ever tried putting yours up, to see how you'll look? Let's do it one day, both of us, and go down and give them a shock, shall we?"

"I perceive," said Joy solemnly, from the doorway, "that we have taken a chatterbox into the bosom of the family! Do you go on like this all the time, Rosamunda?"

"I'm afraid I do! Do you mind?" Rosamund laughed, but looked apologetic and a trifle anxious.

"I like it!" Joy assured her seriously. "You see, I do it myself, and so does Jenny-Wren. So do all the rest of our crowd, so you won't be any shock to us. However much you talk, I don't think you'll out-talk *me*! I'll race you to the teapot!"

During tea, Maidlin sat in her corner, silent, puzzled, suspicious, listening in stunned, incredulous amazement to the chatter of the other three. Was it possible that Rosamund had not been in the house an hour? Maidlin watched and listened, and formed her own conclusions. She did not utter them, but the results were soon apparent. She withdrew into a shell of silence and shyness, sat in a corner with a book while Rosamund, calming down, worked steadily at the big table for two hours; was as silent during supper as the rest were lively, and cried herself to sleep that night.

"Well, Wild Cat? Good hunting?" Jen inquired, when Joy came to brush her hair and talk. "Satisfied with your new family?"

"No, I'm just sick about it!" Joy said vehemently. "I've done my best, and here's the result! Rosamund, who's only supposed to be staying here for the good of her health, is as much at home in half an hour as if she'd been here always. Maidlin, whom I'm supposed to be bringing up nicely, is in the sulks, and hasn't a word to say! And it *isn't* my fault!"

"No, it's the difference between them. They couldn't be much less alike. But so far as I've thought it out, Joy, the difference is a good thing, and, of the two, I'd rather have Maidlin."

"Go on," Joy mocked. "Tell me all about Maidlin. Am I to be glad she's sulking, did you say?"

"She's not sulking. She's frightfully unhappy and lonely, and feels left out of everything. I should have thought even you could see that! Maidlin sees this other girl come butting in, knowing just how to fool about with you, and she feels more awkward and more out of it every minute. I shouldn't wonder if she's been crying in bed to-night. It's been a gloomy evening for poor Maidlin! In time she'll thaw, of course; but in the meantime you simply mustn't go thinking she's sulky, when she's feeling so sick she can't speak!"

Joy whistled under her breath. "I see your point. It's a good thing you're here to keep me straight, Jenny-Wren! But how can I help her?"

"Be nice to her, and wait!" It was Jen's way of pleading for patience and gentleness. "She is worth it, Joy! The very fact that she feels it all so deeply shows she has a lot in her."

"It is rough on her," Joy agreed slowly. "Will the few days in town help, Jenny-Wren? She'll be alone with us then."

"Yes, I think it will. She'll see you're as friendly with everybody—Jack, and the dancing lot, and all that crowd—as you are with me and Rosamund, and that there's no sense in being jealous; that it's just your way. And she'll get to know us better."

"And, of course, Rosamunda will be away at school most of the time," said Joy thoughtfully. "Maidlin can have her innings then. It's a good thing she has to go with us to town; we'd have had to take her, in any case. For we couldn't have left her here!"

"Help, no! Not in the present state of things! Wouldn't it have been fearful for her and Rosamund alone?"

"Well," said Joy, "I'll go to my own little bed. Thank you for your kind advice, Mrs. Wren! Why you should know so much about people's inner feelings and hidden thoughts is more than I can tell! At your age, too! Now I," mournfully, "I never see anything till it hits me on the nose."

"Oh, go to bed, silly!" Jen laughed, and switched off the light, and left her to find her way to the door in the dark.

CHAPTER XV

THE PIXIE AND THE CLUB

"I HAVE to break it to you, Rosamunda, that you will be alone with aunty for two nights," Joy said weightily on Wednesday morning. "Be nice to her, won't you? If she were perfectly honest, I shouldn't wonder if she'd say she's quite glad we're all going up to town for two days. But being so polite and kind, I dare say she'll say she expects to be lonely without us."

"I shall miss you all fearfully!" Rosamund wailed. "Bother your old party! Why must you go to parties in town?"

"To wear our ultra-swish frocks, my child," said Joy.

Rosamund went off to school on Wednesday morning lamenting her coming loneliness, and after lunch the three girls, with a considerable amount of luggage, packed themselves into Eirene, and sped away across the hills to town.

The decision to go to town on Wednesday had been made after Joy had spent Tuesday morning ringing up people and making arrangements.

"Come and have tea with me on Wednesday!" the Pixie had said. "I'll show you my room, and the club, and if you can wait you shall see my men. They come to me for morris, and they're frightfully keen." So Eirene sped hooting through the West End, on past St Paul's and the Bank and the Monument and London Bridge and the Tower, and dived into the unknown crowded whirl of Aldgate.

Even Joy, though born a Londoner, knew nothing of this end of the City. She asked her way of policemen occasionally, but for the most part found it by means of a certain sense of direction which rarely failed her. She knew she had to go east, and east she went, and had no difficulties till Whitechapel lay behind her and she was heading for the river and the docks.

"I've a bump, you know; a bump of locality. I always had," she said briefly, as Jen commented admiringly on her unhesitating decision when they came to a choice of roads.

She pointed out the well-known places they passed, for Jen's benefit as well as Maidlin's, but explained frankly that she only knew the outside of places like St. Paul's, and that only from picture post cards.

"You can't mistake it, of course. But I've never been inside, so far as I know; nor in the Tower. Now we must be getting near the club. Is this the kind of place the Pixie's teaching folk-dancing in?"

And they looked at the crowded streets, and the unemployed men standing at the corners, the squalid houses, the mud and dirt and bustle, with startled eyes.

"Is this the place we sent the daffodils to?" Jen murmured. "I wish I'd sent more!"

Joy was frowning, though not over difficulties of the road. "We ought to know more," she said shortly. "I feel a pig. Did you see those children? Think of our orchard; and those daffodils! Think of our lawns and fields! We ought to help; she'll tell me how."

Maidlin glanced at her in wonder. This was the Joy she loved best; though the other, happy and full of jokes and fun, was a bright and beautiful person to be worshipped from afar, in awe tinged with bewilderment. She began to be curious about this other person, this "Pixie," who was so full of wisdom.

"Will I be afraid of her?" she asked doubtfully.

Joy's lips twitched. "I don't *think* so!" she said gravely. "Will she, Jen?"

"If she is, she ought to have first prize for being a nervous, silly little object," Jen said severely. "Maidlin, you really mustn't go about expecting to be afraid of people! Afraid of the Pixie!"

"Well, I don't know her!" Maidlin was roused to defend herself. "And if she's so clever——"

"She knows everything!" Joy said solemnly. "Every mortal thing you can think of! I'd take her advice about anything."

"Joy, don't tease the kid. You'll love the Pixie, Maidlin. I say! Doesn't it strike you two that a country-dance club for men and girls down here, in the middle of all this, is rather a fine idea? I love the thought of dancing clubs down here. Oh, what's that big white place?"

"I shouldn't wonder if it's the club we're going to, considering the picture she showed us last week."

"Why, it's a palace! How—how gorgeous for the people living round about!" and Jen stepped out of Eirene and stood gazing up at the great white building in delight.

Maidlin followed her in an amazed dream. She had never imagined a "club" of this size, even in fashionable London, let alone in the slums; her only experience had been of a village club-room and small parish hall.

"It's a gorgeous place! I wonder if she'll take us over it? She said, turn to the left, and we'd find her in the restaurant at four-thirty. Oh, here it is!" and Joy pushed open a swing-door and led them in.

Maidlin gazed eagerly round the big hall, with its high windows, little tables, and brown woodwork. Then she looked anxiously, and still a trifle nervously, for the great person in whose wisdom Joy had such faith, the Pixie.

"Here she is!" "Here you are!" the greetings rang out together, and the Pixie ran to meet them.

"So you've found me all right! Did you have any difficulty? *Good!* It is nice to see you here! Isn't it a beautiful place? You must see it all presently. But first we'll have tea. Tea, toast, and bread and butter and cakes for four, please, Beatrice. And is this your new abbey girl? I know all about you, you know," to staring Maidlin.

Maidlin was staring, indeed. She had vaguely expected some one imposing and awe-inspiring, though she could not have said why. This little person was no taller than herself, though she had enough to say for two.

"And how are you getting on at the abbey? Oh, I say, thank you so much for the flowers! Did you help to pick them for me? I know you did!" to Maidlin, who suddenly felt glad that she had helped. "It was beautiful of you all to think of it. Everybody had some; every single person I saw yesterday."

"I've come to ask advice, as usual, Pixie," Joy said.

"What's the trouble now? What's the worry, Joy?"—the keen eyes had seen that Joy was in earnest.

"What ought people like us to do for people who live in those streets we just came through?" Joy asked bluntly. "I feel as if I ought to chuck everything and come here and work with you. You're doing a big thing for the people who live here; anyone can see that. But I couldn't teach! But it seems so hateful and—and callous to do nothing!"

The Pixie looked at her thoughtfully. "The last thing in the world you have to do is to 'chuck everything.' That's not what the money was given to you for. You can do far more by using it properly. By living at home, and asking some of our people there to share it with you, you'll do far more than by living here. You're going to use your house and money for other people. I don't say you can't do something here, too. You can do a lot; and if you'll come and see us often, and join in what we're doing, and be friendly and one of us, it will be a big thing. And a very real bit of help you could give would be to bring Eirene down now and then, and take some of our cripple children out for a ride. Think how they'd love it!"

"Yes, I'd like to do that! Shall I come once a week?"

"And stay the night with me, when we're settled in our flat, and go to classes at night!" Jen said joyfully. "Oh,

Joy! What a lovely plan! You must come on Fridays, for those are the best classes! Except when there's a party; then you'll come on Thursday!"

"I wasn't thinking about classes, or any fun for myself!" Joy said indignantly.

"No, of course you weren't," the Pixie said soothingly. "But there's no reason you shouldn't have it," she added practically.

CHAPTER XVI

A MORRIS PIPE AND A PIXIE

"I'VE no words left!" Jen said weakly. "I've used them all, three times over! It's the most gorgeous club I ever saw!"

Pixie had led the girls to the beautiful gymnasium—"We dance here, on party nights. I play for them, up there!" pointing to the piano on its platform under the roof—to the billiard-rooms, with their big green tables and low, shaded lights—"Anyone can have a game here by paying a little. It's not only for club-members"—to the big lounge and reading-room, the boys' club-room and the girl's club-room, with their huge red-brick open hearths, restful brown wooden furniture, big red leather easy-chairs and settees, tables, with papers and magazines, and cosy corners arranged for discussions;—to the cinema-theatre; and last of all to the big swimming-pool, used during the day by schools of the neighbourhood and at night apen to members of the clubs.

"Cheers for the Y.M.C.A., *I* say!" said Jen, as they came to rest at last in the Pixie's upstairs office.

"Yes, isn't it a wonderful thing for the people down here? And they love it so. All our clubs are full. We could do with another place as big, and still take in more. Now I've got to change; it looks more business-like." And she hurled her garments at them, and in five minutes had changed from her silk jumper to a smooth little black tunic and cream blouse, and was once more the Pixie of the Cheltenham School.

"What do you do for music up here, aunty? You said your men came here for morris. But you've no piano!" said Joy.

"I play for them myself," said the Pixie. "I have my pipe, you know," and she took up a tin whistle.

"Oh, play to us! Do play to us! We didn't know you could!" Jen cried delightedly, and Maidlin's eyes kindled.

The Pixie, in her tunic, perched on the edge of the office table, and began to pipe; and Jen, in the midst of her enjoyment, treasured this new picture for her letter to Joan.

"Here they come! You'll have to tuck yourselves into corners, if they all turn up. Maidlin, you can sit on Jen's knee in the big chair."

Deeply interested, Jen and Maidlin sat in the big leather chair and Joy perched on the arm, while half-a-dozen lads came in, overcome with shyness and amusement at sight of three girl visitors at first, till the Pixie's welcoming chatter made them forget themselves and the strangers. Conscious that they had faded into the background, the girls watched in absorbed silence.

"How they love it!" Jen whispered. "Isn't it wonderful to see them? This is the real thing, Maidlin; real men's morris, even if they are just beginners! It's got life in it; it's tremendously real. And one or two of them are jolly good!"

"Yes, that leader's rhythm is wonderful," Joy too had been watching enthralled. "And others are getting hold of the idea. But we really must go," and Joy rose resolutely. "I could sit here and watch all night, of course, but we simply mustn't. You'll have to show us the way down," to the Pixie. "I'm hopelessly lost in this mansion!"

"I'll take you into the girls' lounge, and anyone will show you the way down. I must hurry back to my men, though. Molly!" They had entered the big lighted girls' lounge. "Show these friends of mine the way down, will you? They're afraid they'll get lost. Thank you, awfully! *Good*-bye! I'll ask you to a party some day!"

Maidlin sprang to hold open the swing-door for her. The Pixie paused to say a word of thanks. "You'll come again, won't you? If you learn a few dances, you shall come to a party too. And see you're nice to that other girl. Remember you were one of the family before she came. You have to do your share in making her feel at home. Now, good-bye, everybody!" and she ran down the steps to her own room, a tiny, eager figure in fawn knitted coat over smooth black tunic, black band round smooth fair hair.

"Darling!" murmured Jen, as Molly led them across the lounge, where girls were sitting at tables or in corners standing round the piano.

"That's all very well!" said Joy sombrely, when they were racing in Eirene through the crowded brilliant streets back to the City and so to the west. "But I want to say more than 'Darling'! Think of what she's doing, just by being there, just by existing, just by meeting those people every day! It would be worth their while to pay her to stay there, even if she never taught a class. Just to have somebody about, thinking and talking as she does, is a big thing. I'm just sorry there's only one of her. She ought to be multiplied by umpteen thousands. There ought to be one of her in every street!"

"Oh, Joy!" Jen laughed. "But I do agree! Oh, that morris pipe, and her perched on the table! I'm dying to tell Joan!"

CHAPTER XVII

EDUCATING MAIDLIN

"SHE's a bit stodgy, isn't she?" Jack said doubtfully.

Jen looked expectantly at Joy, and Joy did not disappoint her. "No, she's not a scrap stodgy!" she said shortly. "It's only that she doesn't understand us, and hasn't learnt how to fool about yet. She's never been with people who turned into noisy lunatics every now and then. Well, what's the matter with *you*?" as Jen gave a shout of laughter.

"Joy, you are funny! You won't have a word said against your infant by anybody else, will you? So you're giving Jacky-boy the benefit of all *my* arguments, that I used to you two nights ago! 'Traveller's Joy,' it's really awfully sweet of you to speak up for Maidlin like that, when you know you don't understand her yourself!"

Joy's first wrath at this betrayal gave way to a merely indignant laugh. It was difficult, for her, at any rate, to be really angry with Jen. "Jenny-Wren, you're a little beast! Why do you need to go and give me away like that? Besides, you're not fair. I spoke quite honestly, meaning every word; I forgot you'd said it all first. You make it sound as if I'd just said it for argument, to crush Jack."

"Oh, but I never thought that! I know you meant all you said. And I do think it's nice of you to stand up for her. She is hard to understand!"

"I'm trying to get to see her point of view," Joy rose and stood before the fire. "Some people know by instinct what other folks are feeling and what to do to help them. You do fairly well, Jenny-Wren! And the Pixie, now; I love to watch her with people, bossing a crowd, and saying the right thing to everyone. That's why I took Maidlin along. I'm curious to know if she'll have anything to say about her. I told the Pixie how difficult Maidlin was, and she said, 'Try to get to see her point of view.' I'm going to try. And to give the kid a chance I'm going to bed now, in case she wants to unburden herself when it's dark and there's nobody there but me! You children can sit up and babble and yatter as long as you like! I'm going to bed with my infant. Good-night!"

"Joy's an awfully good sort," Jack said.

"She's one of the best, and she's getting better every day, without any idea she's doing it," Jen said. "Let's go upstairs, anyway, Jacky-boy! We can talk in bed. I don't say we'll go to sleep, but we might begin getting undressed!"

Joy said nothing when she went into her room, but only switched on one light, as far from the bed as possible, and undressed quietly. But when she was slipping into bed, Maidlin turned towards her at once.

"*You* think *I'm* queer!" Maidlin burst out, and Joy wished Jack could have been there to take back that "stodgy." "I know; I've seen! I've seen you look at Jen, when I sat in a corner and couldn't think what to say, and Rosamund could talk and laugh and play about, as you did. I—I'm two people, like Jen said you were; and—and neither of them's your kind!"

"Oh, Jen said that, did she?" Joy laughed. "I'll ask her what she meant by it! Jen's two people herself, Maidlin; or more than two! Jen's a tomboy, and great fun; she's grown up with big brothers at home, and lots of girls at boarding-school, and she's used to being one of a crowd, and jolly and noisy and happy. And yet she's understanding, and artistic in all her thoughts, and musical; and she's done a lot for the children in the frightfully lonely village on the moors where she lives."

"Oh! I didn't know! I hadn't heard about all that. But she is nice! She—she tries to understand. I *can't* say things! They're all shut up inside me!" Maidlin panted, expressing herself with difficulty even now. "I don't know why. I feel things, and think things, but I can't get them out. You all say such a lot, and it sounds so easy! Aunty and Uncle never talked a lot, or laughed much, or made jokes, as you do. We never said things we didn't mean; you do it all the time!"

Joy laughed. "You poor kid! It has been hard on you to be plunged in among us so suddenly! And the other part of you is the Italian side, I suppose? The side that flares up like gunpowder, and makes you do and say things you'd never thought of before?"

"I can't help it!" Maidlin whispered. "I don't know when it's going to happen. It is just like being two people, Joy!"

"Of course it is! And one's your daddy, and one's your English mother, and they've each made a bit of you. What you have to do, kid, is to find the best bits of both. And how did you like the Pixie? She's a dancing teacher, you know; she teaches it because she feels it's good, and a help to people, and will make them better and happier and more friendly."

"I loved her! I couldn't say it, but I'd —I'd like to help her, like you said you'd try to do."

"We'll help her together," Joy promised seriously. "You shall talk to the lame children when I take them out driving."

"I couldn't. I wouldn't know what to say."

"Oh, yes, you will! You'll soon get into the way of it!" Joy said helpfully. "Must feel funny not to know what to say! And you've not only got to learn to get things out, but to keep them in too! You can't think how awful I felt when you flew off in a temper because I'd brought Rosamund home! It was fearfully unkind to *me*, you know! I'd brought her to my house, and you made it awfully awkward for me, and difficult for me to welcome her properly. You simply mustn't go doing things like that!"

She had felt Maidlin's jump of surprise, and had talked on purposely to give her a moment for recovery.

When she paused, a shamed whisper came at once. "I am sorry! I don't know what made me do it. She's—she's very nice!" bravely. "And she's heaps cleverer than I am."

Joy only said gravely, "I don't know about that. Rosamund's just a usual kind of girl. But she wants to be friends with everybody, and she doesn't understand you yet. You want to learn to fool about, as Jen and Jack do; weren't they idiots at dinner? I say, would you like to start at once? It would be frightfully mad, and an awfully improper thing to teach you; but it would be frightfully good for you!"

"How? What? What do you mean?"

"You're wide awake! It can't do you any harm. Listen, then! Bring your pillow, and any cushions you can collect, and we'll bombard them. I'll take the bolster," and Joy found her slippers, and staggered to the door, the unwieldy bolster in her arms.

Maidlin gave her one amazed, incredulous look. Then she gathered up pillows and cushions and followed, breathless with excitement, to see what would happen.

"It's this room. I guess I know my way about Jackyboy's house by now! Yes, they're babbling; listen!" at a low laugh from within the room. "When I open the door, you fling those pillows one after another, as fast as ever you can. Don't make a sound. Just shy them straight and hard. Oh, good for you!" as Maidlin gave an uncontrollable giggle.

The corridor was in darkness. Joy flung wide the door, and two startled voices demanded sharply, "Who's that?" The light flashed on; but as it did so, pillows and cushions hurtled through the air, and a stifled yell from Jack—"You brutes!"—told that one had got home.

Then Joy, invisible behind the bolster, pinned Jen down on the bed. "Jenny-Wren, I'm two people, am I? Come on, Maidlin! Stifle them both! I owe them one since last August when they nearly battered the breath out of me at Cheltenham! This is R-r-r-r-revenge! Seven months I've waited for my revenge!" she hissed. "Vengeance is sweet! Are you enjoying it, you two?"

"Oh, don't!" gasped Jen, weak with laughter, holding her sides. "Joy, get away! I'm going to die!"

"It's a simply beastly way to behave in another person's house!" Jack spluttered, writhing under the pillows. "As for Maidlin, it's disgusting! She's hardly been introduced yet!"

"I'm introducing her, as hard as I can. Now you may laugh, all you want to! Put that on first, though," and she threw Jack's dressing-gown at Maidlin's head.

"It's simply priceless!" Jen sobbed into her pillow. "Joy talks like a mother about not keeping Maidlin awake late, and then—then this! Joy, you aren't fit to be a mother to anybody!"

"Have you got any jam-tarts, Jacky-boy?" Joy asked gravely.

Jack darted out of the room, a silent barefoot shadow in pale pink pyjamas and tousled black curls. Jen stifled another shriek of laughter.

"Joy, why did you? We don't want them! We've only just had dinner! Maidlin thinks you're mad!"

"I like being mad!" a gurgle came from Maidlin on the floor. "It's—it's jolly nice!"

"Tarts I crave and tarts I must have; they are a necessary part of the entertainment. It's part of the cure," she mumbled in Jen's ear, rolling her over on the bed. "It's working, too. We've broken the ice, I do believe. Don't you see, you ass? We *never* did this with Rosamund!"

"Oh!" Jen came to attention. " 'Traveller's Joy,' how deep and wily you are!" she whispered. "Oh, cheers! Here's the Bold Adventurer come back! What has she brought?"

"Cream buns," Jack explained. "I bought them; they're mine. I meant them for to-morrow night, after the party; but we'll get some more. Come on and make pigs of yourselves! Isn't it a good thing mother's away?"

"If mother hadn't been away, I should have thought twice before allowing Maidlin to amuse herself in this fashion," Joy said maternally. "She was most anxious to give you the shock of your lives."

"Oh, *Joy*!" gasped Maidlin, and Jen and Jack giggled.

The plate, heaped with cream buns, was placed impressively, but rather unsteadily, in the middle of the very dishevelled bed. Jen lay back, limp and exhausted, with all the pillows she could reach thrust behind her back, and held out her hand wearily for a bun.

"I'm weak!"

"Stand by with a sponge!" Joy said anxiously. "Oh, she's not going to faint!"—callously. "But she's far too shaky to eat cream buns safely."

"Such a mad thing!" Jack supplemented. "Don't you wonder Joy ever gets invited out by anybody?"

Maidlin curled herself up beside Joy in a corner, and tucked her feet under a spare pillow. "I've never had a chance to do mad things before. But I like them. I think perhaps I'll do this *often* now!" said she.

"You jolly well won't! I'll see to that!" Joy assured her warmly.

Then the cuckoo on the mantelpiece came out to tell them it was midnight, and the eyes of all four met in conscience-stricken amusement. Joy grabbed a bun in each hand, and rose with dignity. "Thank you for your kind hospitality, Jacqueline! Kindly precede us bearing our pillows, bolsters, and cushions! Our hands are—er—otherwise occupied. Grab two of those buns quickly, kid, or Jen will have taken them all, and then she'll be jolly sick. Lead the way, Jacqueline!"

CHAPTER XVIII

"CUCKOO'S NEST"

WHEN Maidlin met Jen and Jack at breakfast next morning, the vision of pillows, pyjamas, and cream buns that rose before her eyes was irresistible. She broke into an infectious giggle, and Jen laughed.

"And I meant to look so severe! It was simply disgraceful of Joy! Didn't I tell you she was a baby?"

"I liked it!" Maidlin said stoutly. "I like her like that!"

"Oh, you do, do you?" Joy retorted. "We'll see if cream buns at midnight have cured you! Now hustle, infant! We've got a busy day before us."

The day was something of an ordeal to Maidlin, still struggling as she was to get her footing in these unexpectedly deep places.

She was quiet again as they interviewed her father's lawyer by appointment; but Joy was at ease in business of this kind, and the visit did not take long. The great man was interested and very kind.

"All the same, the poor old chap doesn't begin to see through my ideas for you, Madalena!" Joy said solemnly, when they were in the car again and driving towards the West End shops. "Now for your trousseau! Jenny-Wren, you've got to help here. No skulking outside in Eirene when there's work to be done!"

Joy, fresh from trousseau-hunting with Joan, knew where to go; she knew also what she wanted, and what she meant Maidlin to have.

Maidlin's double personality soon showed itself in the matter of choice. At first she turned towards sober, good garments which would wear well—"That would be useful!" she said shyly. And in the next breath, much more shyly,

"Of course, this is lovely! But you couldn't wear it, could you?"

"Why not?" Joy asked bluntly.

Maidlin gave her a startled look. "Why, the—the colour! It's so bright!"

"It would suit the young lady excellently," said the shop-girl, with interest.

"With your hair, and your clear skin, it would be lovely," Jen said decidedly.

"D'you like bright colours, Maidlin?" Joy asked carelessly, a length of flame-coloured silk in one hand, and one of soft grey in the other.

"Oh, I love them!—to look at! But—I never wore colours like that."

"Wait till you go home! To Italy, you know!" Joy remarked. "Don't be so terrified of colours, kid! You're born to them; you've inherited them. Now get over the shock, and tell us just which you like best."

Maidlin's choice, when it was freed at last, was all for colour and richness; for neutral or pale tints she had no use.

"Oh, I *am* enjoying myself to-day!" cried Jen. "I love shopping! Maidlin, do you realise what a boon you are to Joy and me? It's priceless to have the chance of dressing a girl right through, top to bottom, and one who knows pretty things when she sees them!"

"Get into the pink frock while we change!" Joy commanded after tea.

So Maidlin arrayed herself—no lesser word would do justice to her feelings at the moment—in the new dress, and went in shyly to show herself, bright spots of excitement on her cheeks.

Three girls, in business-like blue tunics with green girdle, which they still wore for their old school's sake, were getting into big coats and picking up their dancing shoes.

"Gorgeous," Jack stared at Maidlin frankly. "I love pink frocks!"

"It suits you, Madalena," Joy's tone was carefully off-hand.

"Jolly nice!" Jen looked her over with approval.

Maidlin knew they were satisfied, and her happiness and excitement grew.

Joy's anxiety as to who would be teaching that night had been increasing all day, and Maidlin had heard so much about her hopes that she almost understood. It might be someone referred to as "Madam," or "The Duchess," and in that case Joy was going to be blissfully happy; or it might be one of several others, and anyone else would be a severe disappointment, it appeared.

By Jen's laugh and Joy's groan, she knew the teacher on the platform was not the beloved "Madam," of whom she had heard so much. Jen went forward to ask permission to join in the class.

"Do you mind? We couldn't resist the thought of some morris. If your sets aren't all made up, may we go in a corner somewhere?"

"You squeeze into a corner, and watch," said Joy to Maidlin, and her eyes followed the teacher, whom she had often seen at Cheltenham, as she led a girl out into the middle of the floor and gave her a demonstration of the hop-back step, showed how she had been doing it and just where she had been wrong, and how she could correct the fault.

"Doesn't she take a lot of trouble, just over one person?" Joy marvelled, in an undertone. "I don't know if I'd like to be hauled out and put through it before the crowd like that!"

"You would, if you were keen enough," Jen said wisely. "She knows who are the keen ones, I bet! Doesn't she?" and she looked with a smile at the Writing Person, who had just come in, in big coat and hat and carrying shoes. "Aren't you dancing to-night?"

"I've come for the party. Two hours of party, after an hour of morris, would do me in. I just crawl home as it is.

But I love to watch the classes first. May I ask you something?" to Joy.

"If I may ask something too!" Joy said promptly. "We've brought a kiddy with us; over there, in the corner, with the big eyes! She's been reading one of your books. May I bring her to speak to you? She'll be too shy to say a word, but she'll love to see you. Jen bought the book for her last week, after meeting you on Friday night."

"How awfully nice of you!" the Writing Person laughed to Jen. "I hope she wasn't disappointed in it! I'll go and talk to her while you're dancing. Where are the rest of your crowd? There were a lot of you at Cheltenham."

Joy laughed. "We've been bridesmaids twice since Christmas. Joan and Cicely are both abroad now."

"I am glad! Thank you so much! It's tremendously satisfying to know the end of the story."

"Make up sets for 'Cuckoo's Nest,'" said the teacher on the platform, and the other four with whom Joy and Jen had danced made frantic signs to them to come and take their places.

"Good luck to you!" said the Writing Person. "I've been hauled out into the middle of the hall for this! The capers, you know; she came and worked my arms to show me what she wanted, and criticised my capers at the same time. It was jolly decent of her to think I was worth taking trouble over. I hardly think I am, myself," and she walked down the room to Maidlin's corner.

The girls saw her say something—apparently, "I hear you've been reading something of mine. Which book was it?"—for Maidlin's face lit up in incredulous interest, and they were soon deep in talk.

The class, failing to give satisfaction in its shuffles, found its sets ignominiously broken up and everybody set to practise up and down the room in long lines. Their teacher walked up and down between the lines, watching critically, making comments and suggestions, and very occasionally giving a sparing word of praise.

"She's been telling me about people!" Maidlin whispered to Joy, when the morris class was over, and in the interval the Writing Person had gone to speak to others. "There! That one she's talking to now! She's a Wise Brown Owl; doesn't it sound funny? It means she's the leader of a lot of little children, called Brownies, who aren't old enough to be Guides yet; and she teaches them singing-games, and plays with them, and does Nature-study with them, all in the middle of London somewhere."

"She's the tomboy-girl from Oxford Circus, Joy," said Jen, glancing at the round-faced girl with wavy, bobbed dark hair, who was chatting eagerly with their new friend.

"And that one she's going to now!" as the Writing Person turned to another friend. "She told me about her too," Maidlin said eagerly. "She's the drill and games mistress in a big school, with four hundred girls, and she teaches them all country-dancing, and they dance beautifully. She doesn't look nearly old enough, does she? But then none of them do. I suppose it's the drill dresses, isn't it?"

"And the short hair; that always makes people look younger! I suppose you know everybody?" Joy challenged the writer of books, when she returned from her chat with the jolly, happy-looking gym mistress.

"I wish I did! But I've been coming to classes for some time now, and the same people keep turning up."

"Tell us about some of them!" Jen urged. "We aren't going to dance in this. We're going to race home to change for the party in a moment."

"I'm going out for coffee. I can't go round asking questions of them all, though I'd love to. But I am always interested in the stories lying behind people, of course, and sometimes things come out in talk. One thing that always surprises me is the girls, just bits of girls, who answer to 'Mrs.' when the register's called. That one, first woman in this set, the very pretty dancer; do you see?"

"Yes? She's not married, surely?"

"Got two children, a boy of three, and a girl of five.

Well, she says so!" in answer to their incredulous protest. "I've only seen a photo of them. We asked if she'd been married at eleven, but she was nineteen; it's terribly sad; her husband—an air pilot—was killed last year."

"Tell us some more!" Jen begged eagerly. Joy was listening in deep interest.

"Oh, I can't go on telling life-histories! But there is one very interesting thing about nearly all these people! If you talk to them long, you find they have 'girls' in the background. Sometimes it's the children in their day-school classes; most of them are teachers, of course. But very often it's big girls, Guides, or a club, or Guildry, girls to whom they're teaching folk-dancing in the evenings, mostly just for the love of it."

"And have you girls in the background, too?" Joy asked curiously. "Real ones, I mean? Or are the book ones enough? You don't teach, do you?"

"Not regularly; I wouldn't have the patience! But I have girls too. Mine are a Camp Fire; I've been their Guardian for six years."

"A Camp Fire? What's that?"

"Oh, there really isn't time to tell you that!" she laughed. "But we're very keen on sword and country-dancing. The girls would like morris too, but they can't give the time to practise that I think it needs. My respect for morris is too high, and my opinion of my own is too low. I'd hate to have it badly done. So we stick to swords and country. I remember the excitement the first time I suggested country-dancing!"

"Did you begin it so that you could teach the girls?"

"No, I'm afraid I didn't. That idea came later. I began because I loved the music, and wanted to know what dances fitted the tunes. But the girls were keen from the first. I remember our first night with 'Earsdon,' too," she laughed.

"But if you've taught 'Earsdon,' why do you keep on coming to the class every Friday?" Jack asked curiously.

"For the fun of doing it. I love it, now that I've stopped

being terrified"—Jack laughed sympathetically. "I've got it all written down, and I've taught my own team, and I could teach it again; but I never know how they're all going to turn. I leave that to them; they all know their own places. I always think you need to learn 'Earsdon' at least five times. I say!" she hinted, "hadn't you better—did you say you were going to change?"

Jack gave one glance at the clock, and fled. Joy paused to say to Maidlin, "We shan't have time for any dinner. You can hold out, can't you? It isn't worth while coming with us. We shall simply fling off our tunics and jump into frocks and come tearing back."

"She'll come with me, and have buns in the shop at the corner," said the Writing Person. "You'll come, won't you, Maidlin?"

Maidlin looked up at her with shy interest. "Will you tell me more funny things about your Camp Fire?"

"I'll talk Camp Fire, if you like—Indian names, and gowns, and symbols. You know all about it, of course!"

"It was in the book. I've never heard of it before. I'd like to go camping! Did you ever have a cat just like that one?"

"Grey Edward? We've got him still. He's supposed to be *very* proud because he's been put in a book and everybody's heard about him. He says it doesn't happen to *many* pussies!"

Maidlin laughed. "Does he talk as much as he did in the book?"

"Well, my sister says he does. She translates; he's her cat. We have to take her word for it. Slip out quietly; don't let the door bang. It's a fearful crime. The noise when it bangs nearly reduces Madam to tears," she laughed, to Joy and Jen, who had changed their shoes and were hurrying out. "See you later, then! Come along, Maidlin!"

CHAPTER XIX

ONE JOLLY EVENING

It had been another day of new experiences for Maidlin, but not the least of them came in the last two hours. Hoisted up on to a wide window-sill by Joy, she sat enthralled as the big square hall filled with girls and men, till all the wide floor-space was a mass of moving colour. The dances had no meaning for her yet; she had never seen a country-dance except in that evening's class. Maidlin wondered greatly how they all knew what to do at the right moment, as she saw it happen so easily, time after time. And she saw, without a shadow of doubt, that the dancers were all enjoying themselves immensely; the talk and laughter, and the eagerness for places in sets, testified to that.

She saw the teacher of the previous morris class dancing all through the evening, as if she had not taught for two hours and a half, with only an apple to keep her alive. She saw Joy and Jen dash to welcome another, a brown-haired, happy-looking fair girl in a black evening frock with touches of vivid blue, and bare neck and arms, and heard their greeting, and the jolly, infectious laugh with which she gave them answer.

"Duchess! You've got a new frock! And you *do* look regal in it! Is that because you've got married?"

"No wonder you weren't here to take us in morris, if you were getting into that! We came early on purpose to have a class with you!"

"Have you buried anybody lately?" Madam retorted. "Or do you only do that on Thursdays?"

"Only on Thursdays. So Jen brought me up to town yesterday, for safety's sake. Are you going to dance 'Butterfly' with *him*? For if it's going to be as wild as that 'Haste to the Wedding' on our lawn, I'm going into another set. You two will do some damage indoors."

"We'll be very careful when we come near you and Jen," Madam promised kindly, and went with her husband to a place in the line, and presently danced down the room and up again like a schoolgirl.

Maidlin saw other greetings, too; heard a plump, jolly girl greet Joy with a shout of, "Hallo, Shirley! You've turned up again!"—and recognised her as the heroine of one of Jen's stories; saw Jen rush up a to a black-haired girl of her own age, and, after demanding a dance, begin to talk eagerly about Cicely and Dick, and the two went off arm in arm to find places in a longways set, Jen declaring, "I've never done it! I don't know a step of it. Can you shove me through? Is it fair, or shall I put everybody out?"

"Oh, I'll haul you through. It's as easy as easy," said Avvy Everett, Cicely's new sister-in-law. "It's only 'corners back-to-back, skipping ring of four once and a half round, and change with your partner back to places,' " and this, cryptic as it sounded to Maidlin, seemed to reassure Jen.

"Sure that's all? Oh, I won't funk that!" she laughed.

"What a nice little dance! I love those skipping rings!" and Jen came to rest, breathless and exhausted, on the chairs below Maidlin's perch, where Joy had already collapsed, to pant and fan herself. "Joy, how the Hamlets would love that! We must give it to them soon! How have we missed it so long?"

"Didn't know it ourselves. Yes, they'd love it. We'll have a party and teach it to them, Jenny-Wren. The Club must have a good thing like that."

"I'll fetch lemonade," said Jen. "This is where it would be useful to have a man. Avvy, can't you find a man to scrounge lemonade for us? We're dying! Haven't you any more brothers?"

"Madam dances every dance with a different man, and sends 'em all in turn to fetch lemonade," Joy said enviously. "I'm sure that's the fifth or sixth. She'll be ill!"

"Useful, sometimes, to have all the men buzzing round!" Jen commented, and went to take her turn in the crowd round the table.

"When are you coming to see me?" Madam flung the question at Joy and Jen, as they met her coming down the line in "The Whim."

"When may we? We'd love to. But you're always out. We must go home to-morrow;" they were passing her in the changes of the hey.

"Early afternoon? I'll give you tea! I have that sword class at six, remember."

"We'll love it!" and then they went up the line and she went down.

"If you wait till I write and ask you, you'll wait for ever," Madam called, when presently they met again going in the other direction. "I never touch a pen till I'm absolutely obliged," she said, as she did back-to-back with Joy. "Is that the child who fell out of the pulpit on to us? The Italian heiress? Bring her, too. What have you done to her? I said she was pretty!" as they changed places in the hey.

"Put her into a pink frock. Joy's adopted her, and we're bringing her up and broadening her mind," Jen explained. "Oh, last time!" regretfully, as she bowed and Joy curtseyed.

"Do they often have parties like that?" Maidlin whispered, that night.

The final closing dance, in a huge ring that filled the whole big hall; and other smaller rings inside, till five circles were swinging round at once; the hearty, laughing farewells; the run through the quiet streets; and the hasty but much needed supper, had all seemed dream-like to her, for after the exciting day she was very tired. But it had been a very happy dream, and the music and laughter were ringing in her ears, and the vivid moving mass of colour still danced before her eyes as she crept into bed, less tired in her limbs than Joy and Jen and Jack, who had crawled home "in the last stages of exhaustion and starvation," they declared, but more weary in mind because to her it had all been so new and surprising.

"About nine in the year, in London; three in each term; but they have them at holiday schools as well. I'm simply dead; and to-morrow we'll all be stiffer than stiff! Wait till you hear our groans when we try to go downstairs! Are you wondering why we do it? Because we can't help it; that's all I know. Madam says it's mania; but she's got it quite badly herself. You saw her?—the big, jolly, pretty one, with heaps of friends, who danced *all* the time, and in a way nobody else does, quite. She's asked us to tea to-morrow. Cheers! I want to see where she lives. Now go to sleep, infant. I'm too dead to talk!"

CHAPTER XX

MADAM AT HOME

ENTHRALLED and amazed, Joy and Jen and Maidlin stood and looked at the wonderful hand-wrought book, an old French love-poem, which the artist-husband of their loved Madam laid before them.

Joy had exhausted every adjective she knew. Jen, gazing in rapt delight at the tiny miniatures, the larger pictures, the lettering with its beautifully coloured initials, the designs and symbols in the margins, was dumb for a while. Then she looked up at the artist—a very different person from the one who danced so wildly at parties—and said gravely, "It's like the work of the old monks, who lived in cells and cloisters, and had no time for outside, but only lived to make beautiful things."

Madam had been standing watching their delight with satisfied eyes, that had more than a hint of pride in them. As they left the studio and went into the cosy sitting-room, Jen added, to her, "He may fool about and make us laugh, as he loves to do, as much as he likes! But no one who has seen that beautiful work could ever forget. He's a different person altogether when he's talking about his work."

"Oh, quite!" Madam assented, with a laugh. "But when he comes to my Saturday class for singing games, he joins in and plays like a two-year-old, and everybody bucks up and begins to play harder than they've played all term."

"It must be gorgeous to have your house full of your own husband's work!" Jen was wandering round looking at everything, and showing things to Maidlin. "So nice to feel things are all different from other people's!"

"If you come back in the summer, you shall go up on the roof and see our garden," Madam came in with a big tea-tray.

"Oh, have you got a roof-garden? How glorious! Do you grow things in tubs?"

"We plant things in tubs. They don't always grow," the part-owner of the flat came flying in, in a long, white painting-coat, for some tool he had missed, and disappeared again as breathlessly as he had come.

"He won't want any tea. Where will you have it? At the table, or round the fire?" Madam demanded.

"Oh, may we have it by the fire? How that lovely screen reflects the light! May we sit on those cushions? We'll fetch things from the table! The plates can stand on the mantelpiece!"

"I don't suppose I'll ever be strong-minded enough to get out of this corner!" Joy sank down on the huge divan.

"I'll *never* set that table for visitors again!" Madam said indignantly, as Jen flopped in the other corner and also refused to move.

"It's a beautiful table!" they assured her hastily. "It couldn't be more so. But this fire and these cushions are one shade more beautiful still. We simply can't resist them. Nobody could!"

"Besides, we aren't visitors. You've made us feel far

too much at home," Jen added. "It's the homiest home I ever saw."

"It hasn't a bit the feeling of a newly-married flat," Joy remarked. "And yet you've only been here a few months. How do you do it?"

"It's because we didn't get new things. We both had some, and they were all old. And we picked up other old things, or had them given to us. I'm afraid it's not very tidy, but we both work here, you see."

"It only looks lived-in, not spick and span," Jen looked round in approval at the books and papers, knitting and unfinished needlework, painting materials and tools, laid down where they had been last used.

"Do you like housework?" Joy asked curiously of Madam. "We can't quite get used to the idea! Morris jigs and country-dances seem more in your line!"

"I don't do much. I've a very good woman who comes in and does everything. I do a little dusting—sometimes!" Madam added honestly, with a twinkle. "And I'm getting *very* good at cooking," she added proudly, as the girls laughed. "I'm really frightfully domesticated. I cooked a chicken *beautifully* the other day. It was just perfect!"

"And had hot plates and gravy and everything, all ready at the right minute?" Joy teased.

"*All* ready, at the *right* minute!" Madam assured her haughtily.

Jen had been gazing again round the home-like living-room, and as they said good-bye presently, the thought in Jen's mind forced itself to utterance.

"It was simply awfully good of you to let us come! We hadn't any decent background for you before—only class-rooms and school halls, and we like you far too well for that. We'll always think of you now in these gorgeous, warm, artist surroundings, with all the lovely colours! It's a proper setting for you at last. I think," Jen added pensively, "I think *I'll* find an artist husband, and live in a bandbox flat, all squeezed close together, at the top of a high flight of stairs, in a quiet West End street, and have a roof-garden looking over half of London! And he shall decorate every corner of it for me, with lovely colours, and have nothing ordinary, and nothing that matches anything else; and then I shall feel picturesque and unusual too! Joy, your big old Hall will feel like a barn after this cosy little place! This is like a nest at the top of a high elm tree!"

"It's just perfect!" said Jen, as they set out in Eirene for their long drive homewards through the dark.

"Maidlin, my infant, you're very quiet! Anything wrong?" Joy demanded. "Didn't your tea agree with you? Don't pretend it's shyness with Jen and me, after the cream-buns-and-pillows incident! Didn't you like Madam?"

"Yes, I liked her. She's kind. She was nice to me," and then Maidlin lapsed into silence again.

Over her head, the elder girls looked at one another with raised brows. "Overtired with last night?" telegraphed Jen.

"Got a bad attack of Rosamund?" Joy's eyes asked anxiously.

An unexpected question from the unconscious Maidlin startled them both. "Joy, why did you bring me to town with you?"

Again Joy looked at Jen, and Jen at Joy. Joy pursed her lips in astonishment; Jen shook her head helplessly.

Joy, to help matters on a little, said lightly, "To buy you some frocks, and to see that man yesterday."

"Was it only that?" persisted Maidlin doggedly.

She answered Maidlin quietly, definitely, and as simply as she could. "I took you because I wanted you to begin meeting people, and I wanted to be sure it was a certain kind of person you met. Now those people I took you to meet are all big, happy, hearty people, loving music and art and beauty for their own sakes, and giving up their lives to teaching and spreading them. Do you suppose Madam could settle down in her tiny flat, beautiful as it is, and enjoy it, after teaching folk-dancing all these years? She's too full of the love of it; she must go on teaching, and making new people love it too, and go about giving it to fresh people. As for the Pixie, you couldn't help feeling how great she was in every way; I knew that. That's all, Maidlin. I hoped you'd like them. Did you?"

"Oh, yes, awfully! They're all nice and kind. But I—I thought perhaps there was something else."

Joy looked at her quickly. "Now what are you getting at? Did I show you anything else, besides what I've said? I mean, did you find anything else for yourself in town?"

But Maidlin had lapsed into shyness again. "I—perhaps I'm silly. I'll tell you later, if I can. I'd like to think about it some more first."

Joy looked across at Jen again in amused agonised curiosity. Jen plunged to the rescue. "Joy, when are we going to give those two new dances to the Hamlets?"

Maidlin, finding herself ignored, breathed more freely, and listened with interest.

"Jenny-Wren, you are touching a sore spot; a secret sorrow!" Joy said gloomily.

"Oh? I beg pardon!" Jen laughed. "What's the trouble?"

"My conscience pricketh me sorely, that's all! I've been a slacker as regards the Club. I felt it acutely when that Writing Person talked about teaching her girls, and about the others all teaching their girls! The Hamlets look to me for help now and then. The older Queens, and Joan, are all married and gone; Mirry and Marguerite have each a kiddy, and Cicely and Joan are abroad. I'm the oldest Queen left who can be any use to the Club, in the way of giving them parties, teaching new dances, and all that; and I haven't been doing it, woe is me!"

"Oh, but you've been fearfully busy with Joan's wedding, 'Traveller's Joy'!"

"I know; they understood that. But now that's safely over, they will expect me to do something. It came on me last night—in the middle of 'Newcastle,' as a matter of fact—what a pig I was to come up to town and enjoy myself to the very limit, as I was doing, and forget all about the Club down in the country!—What did you say, Madalena?" at a curious sound, a choke, or a chuckle, or a subdued cheer, from the silent person between them.

"Nothing. I—I coughed," Maidlin explained hurriedly.

Over her head, Joy looked again at Jen. Then she went on, "I shall call a meeting for next Saturday afternoon, and give them all tea. If it's fine enough, we'll dance on the lawn; if not, we'll clear the big hall. We'll give the girls the two new dances, and *they* shall all have as good a time as *we* had last night!"

"Good!" Jen said warmly. "They'll love it! Couldn't we teach Maidlin some dances, so that she could join in? We've a whole week! We'll tear Rosamund from her homework some evening, and have dances on our own!"

"You won't have to tear very hard, if I know Rosamunda at all!" Joy laughed. "Will you learn morris and country-dances, Madalena?"

"Oh, could I? I would like it. It didn't look hard; only a lot to remember!" Maidlin said doubtfully.

Joy laughed. "Of course, you can learn. Right-o! You shall! And we'll show you what *we* can do in the way of folk-dance parties!"

"Cheers! I'm all out for parties!" Jen laughed happily.

CHAPTER XXI

MAIDLIN THINKS FOR HERSELF

"HERE'S a peaceful domestic picture for you, 'Traveller's Joy'!" said Jen. "Aren't you glad to come home, after all? I apologise! It isn't a bit like a barn. It's a dear old house, and I love every stone of it!"

"And a barn's a very jolly place, as the Hamlet Club knows," Joy looked over her shoulder, as she peeped in at the window, where the curtains had not yet been drawn.

Eirene had been pulled up quietly before the big door, and no raucous hooting had as yet disturbed those inside. Mrs. Shirley sat in the corner by the big open hearth, busy with delicate white netting, her white hair framed by the black oak of the settle. Rosamund bent over her books at the round table, the light touching her yellow plaits with gold.

"Yes, it does look homey," Joy said quietly. "I wonder why *I* should have had so much? I'm afraid Rosamunda won't get much more work done to-night. I suppose," and her voice dropped, "we'll have the same kind of uncomfortable time we had before! I don't suppose Maidlin will rise to anything better all at once. Nothing's happened to change her."

"But you never know what's going on inside Maidlin!" Jen murmured. "Look how silent she's been for the last hour!"

"Getting scared of Rosamund again—I say! She's gone! She can't have got the wind up and raced off as she did before, surely?" Joy cried in dismay, finding Eirene empty.

Jen, with quicker intuition, caught her arm and drew her to the big door, which stood open, for their arrival had been expected. Maidlin was just slipping through the inner door into the big warm entrance-hall. Unseen by her, the elder girls caught the door as it swung back, and followed.

To Maidlin's sensitive, shy Italian soul an ordeal lay before her; but to her sturdy, honest north-country nature there was only one thing to be done, and she had the courage to do it. She had been thinking about it and facing it steadily for the last hour, asking no help even from Joy, but she had never hesitated as to its necessity, and she did not falter now.

"Rosamund, I was just horrid when you came. I was a pig, and I'm sorry."

Rosamund looked up from her French verbs in blank amazement. "Oh, how you made me jump! Oh, but you weren't, Maidlin! You were only shy!"

"I wasn't shy," Maidlin said bluntly. "I was angry, because you could play and talk with Joy and Jen, and I couldn't, and I felt bad because I was left out."

"I'm awfully sorry you felt bad," Rosamund said eagerly. "Have you had a good time in town? You've got a new coat! And a red frock! How gorgeous! Let's see it!" and she unbuttoned the big coat with eager fingers.

Maidlin gave a little laugh of relief that the ordeal was over and friendly relations were established.

"I've got heaps of new frocks!" she said, her tone one of shy importance. "I wore a pink silk one for the party. Oh, Rosamund, it was a lovely party! I do wish you'd been there!"

"I'm weak and limp with astonishment!" and Joy tottered to a chair. "Madalena, you do—you do take the biscuit! Why didn't you give me warning?"

Maidlin looked at her doubtfully. Then she turned to Rosamund again. "One night, when the cuckoo struck twelve, we were all eating cream buns on Jack's bed. Joy and I had been pillow-fighting her and Jen. And last night it was striking twelve again as Joy got into bed. We've had a gorgeous time!"

Jen went off into a peal of laughter at sight of Mrs.

Shirley's horrified face. "Maidlin, *dear*! You'll get yourself sent to bed early for a week, to make up for it!"

"I'm green and blue with envy!" Rosamund wailed. "You'll have to tell me every single thing, to make up for missing it all, Maidlin. And I've gone to bed at nine each night!"

Joy sprang up from the chair into which she had pretended to fall, and went to kiss Mrs. Shirley. "I very nearly swooned! But those children will be all right now, thank goodness! Everything gone well, aunty, dear? Oh, a letter from Joan! Cheers! Jenny-Wren, come and hear all the news!"

"How have you managed to bring about this happier state of affairs?" Mrs. Shirley asked in a tactful undertone, glancing at the two girls talking hard beside the table.

"Aunty, dear, I haven't the foggiest notion! You saw how astonished I was. I nearly died of surprise. We hadn't the slightest warning."

In spite of Mrs. Shirley's wishes and advice, that was another late night for all the girls. There was so much to be told, so much to be shown. Joy had to glance at the letters which had arrived during her absence, though they could not be answered till the morrow. Rosamund's endless questions had to be satisfied, and there was a thrilling and extremely noisy half-hour after supper, when all four girls gathered in Maidlin's room, and the parcels were unpacked and their contents spread on the bed. Rosamund's shriek of rapture over the pink silk frock brought Mrs. Shirley in to look also, and the other purchases still to come were described in detail by Jen, while Rosamund listened enviously.

"I wish someone would die and leave me a fortune!" she sighed.

"There's one thing we haven't thought of," Joy remarked as they turned over the white dainty undergarments. "But it's better it shouldn't come from a shop, after all. We'll get the stuff in Wycombe, and Maidlin shall help to make it herself. A country-dance frock, you know. What colour will you have, Madalena? Now!"—sternly. "Say what you'd really like, remember! We've told you what colours you can wear!"

"Pink again, like the Pixie's almond-blossom, Maidlin?" Jen queried.

"No, my best frock's pink!" the practical temperament found utterance. "I'd like yellow," Maidlin said sturdily, "the goldy colour of a daffodil's trumpet."

"Good for you! Golden it shall be. We'll run down to town on Belinda and choose it on Monday. Rosamund, my child, is there any hockey match or other event at school to-morrow week?"

"Not so far as I know. Babs was speaking of a Club meeting to vote for the new Queen. It's time we chose her."

"Cheers! Couldn't be better. We'll ask them here. We'd decided to have a party that day, unless it clashed with anything at school. Who will be the new Queen?"

"I haven't an idea. I don't think anybody has."

"Not the Maid of Honour? I don't know her, but she's a great chum of Babs Honor."

"No, she's leaving, so she can't. I don't know who it will be; there doesn't seem anybody *quite* good enough!"

"We'll send a message to Babs on Monday, then, and notices to the old members. And then we'll have our work cut out for us, between making Maidlin's daffodil frock and teaching her enough dances to get on with!"

"I—I want to say something to-night, Joy!" said Maidlin at bedtime.

Joy had been waiting and hoping for this. "I'll come when you're in bed, then. No, I'll come and do your hair for you."

"Is it about you and Rosamund?" she asked curiously, half an hour later, as she brushed out the thick black mane, her own hair shaken loose and hanging down.

"That's only part of it. It's what—what I thought you had taken me to town for."

Joy's interest deepened. "Yes? Tell me!"

"I thought you wanted me to see how—well, how everybody who felt they'd got something very nice tried to share it with other people! Like passing on that dancing, you know; those teaching people all do it; and the girls in the classes go away and teach other girls; and the Pixie, giving it to those men. They all give it to somebody, because they like it so much. You and Jen do it too!" Maidlin was warming to her subject and spoke vehemently, without noticing Joy's curious intentness of look. "You had a super time last night, and the first thing you both thought of was, how could you give the Hamlet Club a good time too? You thought of it while you were dancing, you said so; in the middle of the dance you call 'Newcastle.' I nearly laughed when you told Jen, in the car this evening; you didn't seem to see that you were doing just as all the other people do!"

Joy had forgotten to brush, and was staring down at her. Maidlin looked up anxiously, "Do you mind? Mind me thinking about it, and about all your friends, I mean? It is true, isn't it, Joy?"

"Yes, it's true," Joy said slowly. "I'm only wondering that it should strike you so plainly. But you are right! It's one of those times when somebody tells you something you've known all along, but never realised."

"Oh, of course, there's more!" Maidlin said eagerly, overjoyed to find herself understood. It had not been easy to speak out, but she had been sure of Joy's sympathy, if only she could express what she wanted to say. "It's everything! You sharing your flowers with those London people! And letting me come here! Wasn't that why you let me come, Joy?"

"Because I had so much myself that I felt I'd be a rotter if I didn't share it, and there were you, needing exactly what I could give. Yes, Madalena, that's why you came here—in the first place."

"And so I thought you were trying to show me, right at

the beginning, what people who have lots of money or lots of nice things ought to do. I thought you meant that I was to share the things I'm getting, and—and so—don't you see? I'd had all that jolly time in town, and poor old Ros hadn't had any of it, and so I simply had to be decent and tell her all about it when we got back."

Joy began to brush again, very gently, with a little laugh at that unexpected "Poor old Ros," to hide how deeply she was touched. At last she said quietly—

"Maidlin, my child, thank you for all you've said. I'd known it all, of course, but quite unconsciously. And I'm glad you told me; it's rather jolly to feel that you haven't been here a week yet, but you're willing to tell me things like that. Now, good-night, and thank you again! Remember I'm really grateful to you, both for telling me all about it, and for making things so much happier here at home. Nobody could do it but you, you know."

She went away, deeply touched and very thoughtful, and did not even go to Jen's room for a chat that night. And Maidlin crept into bed happier than she had been since the news of her fortune arrived; happier than she had thought she could possibly be.

CHAPTER XXII

"ROS AND MAIDIE"

Joy woke next morning to brilliant sunshine, which in the sheltered grounds of the abbey and the Hall meant warmth and freedom from wind. Sure that Jen would be up and out, and that Maidlin would still be sleeping, Joy dressed quietly, and, glancing into Jen's room, found her guess correct. She slipped on a coat and ran out bareheaded to find her.

As she crossed the orchard, where the plum blossom was just beginning to show, she stopped and laughed. For Jen, in a jumper and a very short skirt, was dancing a morris jig under an apple-tree, a daffodil in each hand instead of a handkerchief.

"Stop, you lunatic!" Joy cried laughing, and going forward to her among the daffodils. "Has the sun gone to your head? Or is it the country air, after your long stay in London?"

"It's everything!" Jen came to a breathless pause. "Just being alive, on a morning like this! I came out to gather daffies for the Pixie's girls, but I've remembered it's Saturday and we can't send them. We'll send her lots on Monday."

"I thought I'd send some regularly, if she says she'd like it," Joy said thoughtfully. "There's usually something we could send that would be a novelty down there, even in winter. I'll tell you another thing you can do for her—for herself! You'll do it better than I should. Write her a long letter about the party, and tell her what everybody wore."

"I'll do it!" Jen laughed. "And I'll tell her about Madam's flat, and The Book! I say, 'Traveller's Joy'! Is the Club going to choose our Rosamund for the next queen?"

"I don't know!" Joy was swinging on a low branch, her hair glowing red in the early sunlight. "They always try to keep it dark from the one they mean to choose! It's meant to be a surprise! If they meant Rosamund to be the queen, every one of them would tell her they hadn't the foggiest notion who would be chosen. I shouldn't wonder a scrap. Rather nice to have another queen from the abbey," Joy spoke casually, but her gratified tone showed how the suggestion had pleased her.

Then she turned from Rosamund. "I say, Jenny-Wren! That Maidlin! She took my breath away again last night!"

"Oh! Did she explain? Could she? I was sure there was something behind, but I didn't know if she'd be able to get it out. Tell me, then, 'Traveller's Joy'!"

They walked up and down the sunny path by the old south wall, where the peach blossom was beginning to show touches of red. Joy told of Maidlin's vehement explanation the night before, and a little laugh as she repeated the astonishing reference to "Poor old Ros."

"I thought it was something like that," Jen said quietly. "I'm awfully glad she felt it. She is a good kid, you know, Joy; and she is worth while. Suppose you hadn't let Maidlin come here!"

"She'd have gone somewhere else, I suppose. And it might have been better for her."

"It couldn't, because she's so devoted to you. If only you don't disappoint her, nothing could be quite so good for her as being with you," Jen said wisely. "And Rosamund's nearly as bad. She thinks you're the nicest person she's ever met. She said so."

"Here come the children!" Joy grinned. "What's the row? Oh, are we late for brekker? Sitting swinging in the orchard, Jenny-Wren, and keeping everybody waiting! How can you?"

"We thought you were lost!" Rosamund and Maidlin, hatless, came racing through the orchard. "Breakfast's been ready for ten minutes, and Mrs. Shirley's down, and the post's come, and there's a great fat letter from Ceylon!" Rosamund gave all the news in one breath.

"From the President! Come on, children!" and Joy led the wild race back to the house.

That afternoon on the lawn, and that evening in the hall, and many times during the next week, Maidlin had her first lessons in folk-dancing. While Rosamund was at school and the abbey was in its morning quiet, Jen taught her morris steps and movements on the cloister garth, where she herself had learnt them from Joan, and stood over her till she could pass her circles and side-step as correct, according to the standard set up by Madam at Cheltenham.

"Now you'll do! With that much, if you remember it all, you can get through a good big bit of a party!" and Jen allowed her to rest. "Oh, 'Traveller's Joy'! *Do* you remember 'Hey, Boys' at Cheltenham, that first afternoon"?

"Tell us about it!" Rosamund begged. "I love to hear about Cheltenham! Come on, Maidie! We'll go with them next August, shall we?"

"Ros, what a gorgeous idea! I'd love it!" Maidlin spoke fervently. "Joy, would they have us? Would we see all those jolly people again?"

Joy nodded, her fingers wandering into the new "Spring Song," which was still haunting her. "They'll all be there, of course. Cicely and Joan, too. Don't see why you shouldn't go. But you'd better work hard at your morris, or you'll find yourselves with the beginners, while *we* shall be Advanced students!"

"They might get the Pixie to teach them, though," Jen remarked. "She had beginners for the last week last year, Maidie."

"Ros wants to see her, too," said Maidlin.

"I want to see them all! Maidie's jolly lucky."

"Times have changed!" Joy murmured, her lips twitching, as Jen bent over the piano. "Ros and Maidie! Since when?"

"It's a change for the better, anyway," Jen said heartily.

CHAPTER XXIII

"SPRING GARDEN"

MRS. SHIRLEY came down the wide staircase to the entrance-hall, and smiled at the picture of the four girls in their dancing frocks, as they waited for the members of the Hamlet Club to arrive.

In Joy's memory, that afternoon lived as "the party when things happened." It was the most eventful meeting of the Hamlet Club she had known.

All began happily, however, and even Maidlin forgot to be shy as the crowds of eager, bright-faced girls arrived, cycling, walking, or driving, changed their shoes and left their coats and hats indoors, and gathered on the lawn, where a morning's hot sun had dried the smooth turf, and a week of showers and sunshine had brought the spring flowers into full glory.

Mrs. Shirley smiled, as she stood watching from the long hall window. Babs Honor—Queen Barbara—had insisted, for reasons of her own, on opening the dance with Rosamund, and was leading her down the middle. Joy had Maidlin as a partner, and if Maidlin's skipping was a trifle uncontrolled, it was very hearty and full of enjoyment.

Jen was dancing with Nesta, one of her first partners, four years ago. But when "Rufty" was called, she came to claim Maidlin for her partner, and the long lines changed as if by magic into squares for four.

After several set dances, for eight and six, Joy called for "longways for as many as will" again, and, standing on a chair, taught the two new dances she and Jen had learned at the party.

Then came tea, in groups sitting under the trees, on all the rugs and cushions the house could furnish since no one would agree to go indoors; and after tea a time for rest and chat. Joy and Jen, making up for the interval since their last meeting with the Club and greeting friends on every hand, met near the house, and stood on the slope below the windows, looking over the pretty scene.

"Rosamunda's taking care of Maidlin and introducing her to 'dear old Meg' and everybody else. She's a jolly good sort!" Joy said warmly. "And Maidlin's thawing visibly in the atmosphere of the Hamlet Club!"

Jen nodded, but her eyes were on the almond-trees around the lawn—on the green dancing floor, and the hyacinths around its border.

"'Spring Garden'!" she said softly. "Joy, they *ought* to dance it!"

"You'd have to give it them. I haven't even seen it," said Joy.

"I? I couldn't teach the Club!"

"Why not? You teach your classes at home!"

"Oh, but they're only infants! I could never teach the Club!"

"I saw you writing it down," said Joy ruthlessly. "And you know you looked it up in the book, and said it was all right. Don't funk, Jenny-Wren! You'll teach us beautifully!" and before Jen could finish her protest, she was mounted on the chair, and the girls, eager and interested, were in longways sets of eight before her.

Half-shy for once, and very doubtful of her own powers, she eyed them deprecatingly, more than half inclined to apologise for her impertinence. For a moment she hesitated, then laughed, and spoke out bravely.

The dance was complicated and long, for a country-dance, but Jen's orders were very clear and very definite. There were some girls present, however, who would not, or could not, take the trouble to think and remember; and for their sakes movement after movement had to be repeated again and again. At last Jen, exasperated beyond bearing, sprang from her chair and fairly hurled herself into the midst of the offending set, scolding right and left.

"I said turn *right*, everybody! Everybody means *all* of you; don't you understand English? Edna, which *is* your right hand? Go back to the beginning of the figure—the back-to-back square. Not the rest of you; you were all right. It's only this set; they're hopeless, I think. No, *no*, Nesta! *That* way; right round, the longest turn!" and she took her friend by the shoulders and swung her round.

"*Now* do you all see? Very well then! Do it once more, with the music, everybody, and do be careful, or I really shall begin to say things!—What's the matter with you, Joy Shirley?" indignantly, for Joy had collapsed on the grass, hugging herself in silent glee.

"Madam! You've got her style to a T! It was priceless! You're just her over again! Didn't you know? I could just *see* her! I nearly died!"

"Joy, you are an idiot! We're ready, all but Joy, thank you, Margia! Be careful now, girls! Do think this time!"

"Madam's mantle has fallen on you, Jenny-Wren!" Joy murmured, as she took her place by Maidlin again.

Jen ignored her, though she saw well enough. But at the end she said, with deliberate intention, "Yes, that's *quite* good! It really wasn't at all bad! Try to remember that for next time!" and her eyes met Joy's mischievously.

"Visitors, Joy! Alice is looking for you," Maidlin came up as the girls gathered round Margia, clamouring for something simpler.

"Bother! On a Saturday afternoon? I do call that the limit!" Joy said indignantly.

"Must you go? Won't Mrs. Shirley see them?"

"She will, but I mustn't leave it all to her. Joan doesn't like her to be worried, and visitors worry her. They don't need me here. You can carry on all right!" and Joy ran across the lawn to the house, with no very cordial feelings towards the intruders.

CHAPTER XXIV

ANOTHER QUEEN FROM THE ABBEY

"BOTHER! Oh, bother!" Joy exclaimed, as she glanced at the card the maid handed her. "Those people again! Are they always going to catch us at awkward times? What do they mean by coming on a Saturday afternoon, anyway?"—for the card bore the names of the old lady and her son, who had come to see the abbey on the morning after Joan's wedding.

"Their car had a breakdown, Miss Joy, and it was near our gate, so they came in to ask if Atkins could lend a hand at getting it right again, and Mrs. Shirley said the lady must come in to rest and wait."

Mrs. Shirley had sent for tea for Lady Marchwood, and was apologising for her delay in calling. As Joy went forward to add her explanation, the grave eyes of the man standing by his mother were on her curiously; she was so very dainty in the green and white frock.

"I fear we have intruded at an awkward time," Lady Marchwood glanced at the window, where the bobbing heads of the girls could just be seen.

"Oh, that doesn't matter at all, if you'll excuse my dancing frock! We're only having a schoolgirls' party, a meeting of our folk-dance club," Joy said lightly. "Won't you come and watch? It's really rather pretty, especially on the lawn," and she led them to the window.

"It is quite a pretty scene," Lady Marchwood said graciously, as the tea arrived, and she and Mrs. Shirley turned back to the table.

"It's more than pretty. May I watch? I would rather have this than tea. But I must not keep you——"

"I've had mine with the girls. Yes, do watch! I must

wait on your mother first, though. I'll come back," and Joy went to hand tea and cakes.

The voices of the girls, as they sang for their introductions—"If all the World were Paper, if all the Sea were Ink"—put the finishing touch to the picture on the lawn, and the great man's face softened to a smile which changed it surprisingly, as he said—

"Inexhaustible energy! One would think they would have no breath left!"

"The singing's feeble!" Joy retorted. "But after 'Goddesses,' it's no wonder."

"Won't you go and dance with them? I feel we have spoiled your afternoon."

"Oh, I've danced heaps, thank you! I've been taught one new dance—by Jen; and I've taught the rest two others."

"I would like to see more," he said regretfully, as Lady Marchwood rose to go. "Don't you invite friends to look on?"

"Well, of all the cheek! Friends!" said Joy to herself, in indignant surprise. "Not outsiders, as a rule," she said definitely. "We generally dance at school, or in our barn, near Wycombe. This is a special invitation."

"We are neighbours. I hope we must not always remain outsiders," he said tentatively. "Oh, but they are wanting you! We have trespassed on your time too long already!" as a shout went up from the lawn for "Joy! Joy!"

"I ought to go. I expect they want me to vote for the new May Queen. It's a very important occasion!" and Joy excused herself and fled, glad to cut short the discussion of the extent of their possible friendship.

She ran lightly down the dark-walled hall, and at the doorway met Queen Barbara giving out voting papers, scribbled Rosamund's name on a slip, and screwed it up and handed it back to Babs.

A letter was awaiting her on the hall table. She took it up, in curiosity, which deepened as she saw it bore the stamp of the lawyer on whom she had called with Maidlin, ten days before. She tore it open, and glanced at the first few words; then, with a dismayed cry of "Help! Oh, *no*! Not that! Oh, what *hard* lines!" she dropped on the settle, and read the long letter through at feverish speed.

Then, clutching it in her hand, she raced through the house, forgetful of the dancing girls, the new Queen, everything; caught up the key of the abbey gate, and sped away down the shrubbery path and into the abbey, to find Ann Watson.

Ann was just showing out the last party of visitors for the afternoon, for the abbey was not open to tourists after six. They were ladies of the neighbourhood, who had brought friends who happened to be staying with them; and, knowing Joy well, they smiled and stopped to greet her.

"We heard the music, Miss Shirley. Is it a meeting of the dancing Club?"—and the strangers eyed the mistress of the Hall, in her picturesque costume, with interest and felt themselves in luck.

Ordinarily, Joy liked them well enough; but at the moment it was all she could do not to be rude. She answered as briefly as possible, then said good-bye and went into Ann's little sitting-room, and the guests had no choice but to go.

As the big gate clanged and Ann turned to see why she was wanted, Joy met her in the old cloister passage. "Ann, when did Maidlin see her father last?"

Ann gasped at the sudden question. "It's a long time, Miss Joy. Five years, I guess it'll be."

"Five years! Oh, good!" Joy drew a long breath of relief, and leaned against the wall. "Then she can't remember him much. Look here, Ann, he's dead. I've just had a letter from the man in London. Now I've got to go and tell her. She'll come to you, I suppose, since you belong to her; she'll want somebody of her own at first! Now you tell Maidlin that I'm ready to do every single thing I can. She can stop with us till she's grown up, and after, if she wants to. I'd like her to feel from the first moment that she has a home, and that somebody wants her. Tell her I'll stand by her and see her through, as long as ever she needs me."

"Oh, Miss Joy, it's that good of you!" sobbed frightened Ann. "Whatever we should ha' done without your help, I *don't* know! And that's the truth!"

"Neither do I, and that's the truth too!" Joy said to herself, as she crossed the garth soberly. "But I'm not doing it because I have to, and because there's no one else, this time. I hope—oh, I do hope we've made her feel we really want her! For we shall know now. This will show how she feels, when she knows it's for years, not months!" and she went still more slowly, her face very grave.

As she locked the abbey gate, a shout from the lawn startled her and reminded her of the great events in progress there. Looking through the bushes, Joy saw Queen Barbara leap from the chair on which she had stood to announce the result, and fly across the lawn, to fling her arms round Rosamund, who, astounded and unbelieving, was the centre of a cheering crowd.

Joy laughed a little. "How mixed up things are! It's one of the great moments of Rosamund's life; of the early part of it, anyway! And one of the saddest of Maidlin's. How pleased Madalena looks! She's shouting with the best of them; nice kid!"

The girls, in a big ring, hand in hand, were dancing "Sellenger's Round," the reigning Queen and the Queen-elect in the middle. But Rosamund's happy eyes, dazed still with surprise and delight, had discovered that Joy was not in the ring, though Jen was there, dancing as heartily as anyone. Diving under the arms, the new Queen made a very undignified exit as she raced towards the house, shouting, "Joy! Joy! Where are you?"

"What's the hurry, Rosamunda?"

"Oh, Joy, I'm the new Queen! Isn't it simply gorgeous? I never dreamt they'd choose me! Isn't it lovely of them?"

and Rosamund hurled herself into Joy's arms, which caught and held her in warm sympathy.

"Isn't it awfully nice, Joy?" Maidlin, with the same idea, had followed close on Rosamund's heels. "Aren't you pleased?"

"Of course I'm pleased, and frightfully proud!" Joy assured them warmly. "But I'd seen it coming. I thought it was very likely."

"Oh! *I* never did! How could you?" Rosamund cried excitedly.

"Little things had made me think it might happen," Joy said seriously. "It's simply gorgeous, kid! I'm awfully glad. Go and tell aunty! Maidlin, won't we have a topping time helping her to choose her colour, and her flower, and her Maid, and everything? Oh, you must be a red, red rose when you're crowned!"

"I'll think about it," Rosamund laughed, and ran in eager delight to tell the good news to Mrs. Shirley.

"Isn't it jolly? Good old Ros!" Maidlin said happily.

Joy put her arm round her, and drew her down on the settle. "Maidie, the Club doesn't need us for a few minutes. They'll be too busy congratulating Rosamund. I have to tell you something, dear."

Maidlin looked up at her with startled eyes, her sensitive instinct aware in a moment that something was the matter. Joy had never called her "dear" before, nor had she spoken in this very gentle tone, though she had always been kind.

"I've had a letter this evening from that man we went to see in town, before the party, you know. Do you remember the last time your father came to see you?"

Maidlin's bewildered look had deepened. "I do remember, but not very well," she said honestly. "I was only nine, Joy, and—and I was rather frightened of him. Is he coming again?" There was more of dismay than of pleasure in her startled tone, as the idea occurred to her as a possible explanation of Joy's gravity.

Joy's arms tightened round her. "Maidlin, he isn't coming any more, dear."

Maidlin flung back her head and stared up into her face. "Joy! Why?" she whispered. "Joy—oh, what was in the letter, Joy?"

"A story, Maidie," and in as few words as possible Joy told her. "All the white people in the little town got together for safety," she explained, when she had told of the sudden rising of the natives. "They were a very long way from any other white people. There were seven men, and three of them had their wives there, and there were some little children. One man was a missionary, and [illegible] were doctors, and they meant to stay there always and work for the good of the Chinese people, and so they had their families with them. The men who had no women and children, like your father, could perhaps have got away, by disguising themselves as Chinese and escaping to the coast. But that wasn't possible for the wives and children, and, of course, the fathers couldn't leave them. So the rest said they'd stay and help to defend them to the last. When the fighting was all over, one man who had managed to hide, a Frenchman, did get away, and he escaped safely and brought the news. But he knows none of the others could have got away; he—he saw what happened. Maidlin, you must always remember your father wouldn't run away, though he had the chance, because there were weaker people left, and he had to stay and protect them. It's a very fine story, Maidie, dear."

Suddenly Maidlin raised her head. "Joy!"

Joy had been waiting for her to spring up and run to Ann for comfort. She said quietly, "Yes, dear?"

"I've got *you*?" It was a question, and one full of dreadful anxiety. "You won't send me away? I—I haven't any right here, but—Joy, I do want to stay!"

Joy's hug almost crushed her. "Maidlin, that's your right! And I want you to stay! We'll make plans for you together. I think you should go to school with Rosamund, next term. You've seen the girls now, and they know you. They'd welcome you, and you'd have a very good time."

"Joy, where are you?" Jen's voice called her from the doorway. "The girls want you for the last dance; they say you haven't danced in Rosamund's honour yet! Have you heard? Is anything the matter?" She looked at her with quick intuition.

"Yes, a little bit of trouble for Maidlin. But it's going to be all right; don't worry, Jenny-Wren!"

Rosamund came flying across the grass to meet them. "Joy, where's Maidie? Can't you make her say she'll come to school? For I want her for my Maid."

"You must go and ask her, as soon as we've had one more dance, in your honour, Your Majesty!" Joy laughed. "No, don't fetch Maidlin for this. She's danced enough for her first day. Go in the middle with Babs again! And don't run away as you did last time! It was most undignified! You must remember your position now, you know!"

"Oh, but that was to find you! I wanted to tell you first of all!"

"Jolly nice of you! I'm frightfully pleased about it. So's Maidie. Now, girls, 'Sellenger's Round!' And then all go home to bed!"